Trust Me

Luna Mitchell

Contents

Prologue

He slammed his fist down on his desk jarring everything on it. His cold eyes bore down into the man that stood across from him hoping not to show the fear he felt inside. He could not lose control.

"I can't believe he made that move. Didn't I tell you to watch him closely?" The man behind the desk pushed himself up and began pacing. The black of his suit stood out in sharp contrast to the beige walls that surrounded him. Only the bright colored paintings broke up the boredom of the room. The man though was anything but boring.

His suit was expensively cut with gold studs on the sleeves and an emerald tie clasp that sparkled with every movement. His silver hair was trimmed and thick. He was proud of the fact that he had a full head of it. There was no need for fake hair for him. He only had the real thing in everything.

He leaned down over his desk bracing himself with both arms. The other man watching him stood ready to receive the brunt of the other's anger. It was expected. The messenger was the one who got shot especially if they were the one who didn't follow orders in the first place. Instead of anger, he got a very surprising reaction.

Laughter burst from the man as he flung his head back. His eyes danced with mirth. Thin lips stretched into a sadistic smile.

"This will turn out better than I had planned. He's good. He's very good, but not near as good as I am." His eyes met the other man's confused look. "Stay in the shadows. Keep me updated. He thinks he has double-crossed me. What he doesn't know is that I'm one step ahead."

Dismissed, the man walked out of the room closing the door on a laugh that bordered on malicious. It was a sound that followed him down the elevator and out into the busy street. He did not envy the traitor.

Chapter 1

Pulling the hair band out of her hair, Ranalla walked out of the bathroom. Her long, blond hair fell around her shoulders when she shook her head to loosen it from its confines. Dressed in loose shorts and an old t-shirt, she climbed into bed and pulled the blankets up. She was bone tired and couldn't wait for slumber to come. The day had been long and stressful. She needed to just let her body relax.

She reached over and turned off the light. The room was blanketed in darkness. A small glow from a street light reached into her room between her blinds giving her just a small amount of light to see by. She wasn't going to need it as long as sleep called to her.

Pulling up the soft blankets, Ranalla settled down and sighed. It felt so nice to have it all to herself. Everything was beginning to roll smoothly.

She loved her new place.

For six months she had been looking for an apartment to rent. She had only been in the other apartment for a few months when she began to get the feeling that her roommate was going to have her boyfriend move in. The hints were getting to be not so subtle as he walked out of her roommate's room every morning and more and more of his stuff was appearing in the bathroom.

It was hard to find a place on her salary at the bookstore. She made just a little above minimum wage. She sold her car for the cash and to save money on her insurance. Ranalla didn't mind eating cheap, frozen meals. Money for anything extra was not even a consideration. Finding another place was near impossible.

The apartment had just fallen in her lap. Someone had dropped off a flier at the bookstore. When her manager, Donna, saw it, she tucked it away until Ranalla came into work. She had been helping Ranalla look for a place within her budget, but even her extensive network of contacts couldn't turn up anything that wasn't in an extremely bad neighborhood. Donna even thought of creating an apartment in the back of the store, but the landlords would have gotten a tad bit upset with it. Seeing the flier, Donna knew she had to let Ranalla know about it. She gave her the flier and sent her out the door to check it out without giving her a chance to even take her coat off. The price on the paper was too good to be true. Ranalla was skeptical as nothing was ever what it seemed. Nothing ever had in her life. It always came with strings that would eventually become painfully tightening. It could not be real and, even if it was, by the time she got there it would already be taken. She was beginning to accept life as one brick wall after another. There were other ways to solve her problems, but she would rather live on the streets than go back there.

It turned out to be true, all of it. She checked the fine print, even held the contract up against the light looking for hidden traps. She had a lawyer friend go over it. It was perfect. The price was a special and was a first come-first serve basis. She signed the rental agreement as soon as her friend approved it for fear of losing such a great opportunity.

It was a ground level apartment that had its own private yard surrounded by a high brick wall and a locked iron gate that led to a heated garage. It was located in a developing area where all the upscales were moving to. It had to meet their approval. The inside was newly furnished and painted and included top of the art appliances. She couldn't have asked for anything better. It was like she had stepped into heaven.

She had two bedrooms and one large bath. The spare one was quickly turned into a library to house her legion of books. A fireplace took up one wall in the living room which was larger than anything she really needed, but she enjoyed the spacious feel. All that was left to do was add a few touches to make it her own.

She had been there only a month, and it still felt like a dream. As she snuggled down in the bed, she thanked her lucky stars for it. Things were starting to go right for her. Maybe she could shake her past and move forward. She had learned the hard way that having loads of money did not by happiness. To her, it only brought sorrow. Slowly she faded and let the night take her away as she dreamed of the promise the future was giving her.

****

A noise woke her. She turned her head to see the clock on the nightstand; it brightly displayed 2:00. She lay still as she tried to figure out what had made the noise. She didn't have any neighbors on this side of the building, and the apartment upstairs was currently vacant. She had no pets; then again, she wasn't sure the noise had been real. It might have been a dream that seemed real.

A few minutes went by, and she didn't hear anything else. Not even sounds from the streets could be heard. Thinking it was just a dream, she closed her eyes and began to drift to sleep again. Nothing had seemed out of place in the little bit of light that filtered in. All the shadows remained still, all but one that moved at the closing of her eyes.

The hand that clamped over her mouth brought her abruptly from the edge of sleep. Her eyes flew open as her arms and legs began to fight the unknown attacker. All she saw was a shadowy figure above her. Ranalla's hands bent to become claws. For the first time without any vanity, she was glad she had long nails. She began scratching at anything her hands could reach. She felt flesh under her nails for a second. As a curse was muttered, her hands were roughly grabbed. Kicking was removed as an option as the figure straddled her preventing her from using her feet and legs to inflict damage. She found herself unable to make an offensive move. He pulled her arms down to her sides and pinned them with his weight. She continued to fight though it resulted more of her thrashing under him. The face came near her ear. In the dark, she still could not see anything but felt every move made above her. She felt hot breath tickle her skin causing goose bumps to appear on her skin. Fear of the unknown began to chock her. Everything was encased in shadows and the fear building inside of her removed all logic and reason.

"Shhh. Sorry about this." She felt a prick on her arm....

Chapter 2

Ranalla shifted. It felt warm under the covers, and she didn't want to wake up. Sleep was too comfortable and inviting. Slowly the events of the night before returned to her foggy mind. Her eyes shot open as her whole body froze.

Her mind cleared, and she began to assess her situation. She knew she was in a bed. It was a very comfortable bed. Moving her fingers ever so slightly, she could tell the sheets were expensive and soft. The pillow under her head was luxurious as feather down. Her breathing began to even out as she realized she was at least comfortable. Moving her fingers further, she knew she was still wearing the clothes she went to bed in.

Only her eyes moved as she looked around her. She was in a room that resembled the interior of a nicely built cabin. The walls were paneled wood, as was the ceiling. A few pictures were hung on the wall depicting hunting scenes. Light from the sun streamed in through one of the two windows in the room. She couldn't tell much more from where she lay until she moved, but she could see the top of the two windows clearly. The light fixture above the bed was attached to a ceiling fan that was not moving. That was all she could see without moving.

From the amount of sunlight, she determined it was late morning. She didn't detect any musky smells that would accompany an unused cabin. Everything felt fresh and clean, including the sheets she found herself under. It seemed so peaceful and nice.

Her ears strained to pick up any sound in the room. Nothing but the sound of birds through the window could be heard. Sniffing, she smelled fresh linen telling her the sheets had been washed recently. A faint cedar smell came to her from the walls.

Taking a chance, she moved her head slightly. In her line of sight was a closed door. Its dark wood created the only barrier between her and freedom. Her eyes moved on and revealed an open door that led into a bathroom and a closed door that she assumed was a closet. She dare not hope it was her escape exit. The only other furniture she could see was a dresser and a chair as well as a lamp on the nightstand next to her. It was sparse without being barren.

She took in a deep breath trying to calm her racing heart. Ranalla had to keep her wits about her if she was to have any chance of escape.She needed to be calm. It was the only way she'd ever find a way to escape.

A noise from the other side of the door alerted her to a presence. She quickly closed her eyes and focused on keeping her breathing even. Maybe if she pretended to be asleep, she could have the advantage. The door creaked open. Footsteps indicated the entry of her captor. She could detect a slight rustle as jean-clad legs moved against each other. It stopped beside the bed. She could feel eyes watching her.

"You can stop pretending to be asleep," a man's voice, low and husky, spoke from above her. She ignored him and continued to focus on her breathing. Poker was a game she was good at playing. She could bluff her way through this.

"Ranalla, open your eyes."

At her name, her eyes flew open and collided with a pair of coal-black eyes. She stopped breathing. Any other time she would have admired the sexy dark look, but the eyes were those of a kidnapper.

Chapter 3

S he didn't move as she watched the man standing above her. His intense black eyes were set in a chiseled, olive-skin face. His jaw was set as though his teeth were clenched. His dark hair was cut short and had a slight wave to it. She didn't dare look anywhere else. Fear engulfed her as she looked on him. He was a deadly combination of danger and seduction. What did he want?

A smile pulled at the corner of his mouth. "Now that you're awake..." He sat down on the bed next to her. The movement unlocked her frozen body. She scooted quickly to the other side of the bed as the heat radiated from his body. He chuckled.

She watched the amusement in his eyes. He might have thought it was funny, but she was not laughing. Her heart was pounding as adrenaline raced through her veins. A slight roaring sound filled her ears and she could feel her insides shaking.

"I brought you something to eat." For the first time, she looked down from his face. His strong hands held a wooden tray with plates of food on it. Her stomach betrayed her with a loud rumble. "Come on and eat." He set the tray down on the bed between them. Having an object between them made her feel a little better, but it wasn't enough.

Slowly, she sat up while keeping her eyes on him for any sudden movements. He laughed as he watched her move slowly with her eyes glued to him. Her body was tight and ready to bolt for the door, even though she knew she didn't have a chance.

"Don't worry. I'm not going to hurt you. Just eat. You've been asleep so long that you've missed breakfast, and lunch is long past." He moved the tray a little closer to her.

She hesitated as she listened to his voice. It wasn't what she assumed a kidnapper would be. He spoke softly with authority. It appeared he was trying to ease her fears. Ranalla was finding it hard to reconcile her ideas of what his voice should be and what it really was.

Her eyes took in the sandwich, bowl of chips, and the plate of fruit sitting there. Her stomach rumbled again and her mouth began to water at the sight of the food. Unsure of what was happening, she still held back. She wasn't even sure if she should touch the food. It could be drugged so he could have his way with her or make it easier to torture her. There was no telling what was going on in his twisted mind. After all, he had snatched her out of her own bed in the wee hours of the morning.

He was amused at her. As though reading her mind, he said, "I said, go ahead. I didn't poison it."

Gingerly she picked up the sandwich and glanced up at his pleased look. Taking a peek at what she was about to eat, she was pleasantly surprised to see it was chicken salad. It was one of her favorites, which was a relief. It wasn't something gross.

She took a tentative bite, gave in to the delicious taste, and quickly took another. A satisfied sigh escaped her. She paused and looked back at her captor. She had betrayed herself with her reaction to the food. She watched him with wide eyes. Mentally she was kicking herself for letting her guard down and allowing him to see how much she enjoyed the food. That was giving him more of an advantage over her.

His only reaction was a lift at the corner of his mouth. She looked back down at the sandwich. Now that she had tasted the food, she wanted more. She quickly took another bite.

"Good to see you have an appetite." He watched her finish the sandwich and drink the cold cranberry juice.

As the sandwich began to fill her stomach, she took a small bite of the chips. "Why am I here?" She kept her eyes down on the plate fearing what his reaction might be. She did not want to see the evil in his eyes as he informed her of his intentions.

Several moments went by with no answer. She dared to look up only to find him staring back. He watched her with no expression. As she waited on a response, she was able to get a better look at him. She had to admit that he was one to take a second glance at with broad shoulders and muscles. His button down shirt couldn't hide his physique. It demanded attention which made her heart beat all the faster. Mentally, Ranalla shook herself. She didn't need to feel an attraction to the man who had kidnapped her. He was the bad guy.

"Well?" She met his eyes in challenge. The silence was driving her crazy and raising her fear level.

He stood up and walked to the window that was located next to her bed. He pulled the curtain back. The sunlight filled the room as he gazed out into the world beyond, ignoring her.

She raised herself up on her knees. "I asked you why I am here."

He continued to stare out the window. "I heard you." His voice held no emotion.

She watched closely. He took his sweet time turning to her. His eyes drifted down to her tank top and the breasts that were not well concealed. In her anger, she didn't even notice. "You'll find out soon enough." He turned and walked out the door leaving her staring speechless at his retreating back. The door closed with a resounding click as a lock turned. She was a prisoner within this room and still had no idea why.

Chapter 4

According to the clock next to the bed, she was left alone for three hours. During that time, she munched on the rest of the chips and the fruit trying not to keep looking at the slow moving time. Despite herself, her hunger had caused her to clean the tray. She had wanted to appear nonchalant about the food, but her body had betrayed her. It wanted it all and the evidence was before her. She'd just have to face the music and pretend it meant nothing to her.

A bookshelf was located next to the bed and surprisingly offered a wide variety of books. Bored with the food gone, she picked a few up, but none of them grabbed her attention. She was surprised to see most of her favorite authors, but being a captive dampened her desire to read.

She walked over to the window that still had the curtains pulled back and looked outside. All she saw was a small lawn and trees. Nothing gave her a hint of where she was. The other window did not offer up any more clues to where she was located. The scene was the same. Trees blocked the entire view. If there was anyone out there, they would have never been seen. It was as though she was in the middle of a forest.

She pushed on the window. She wasn't even surprised to find both of them nailed shut. Running her hands around the panes showed that they were solidly framed, too.

She tried to get an idea of where she was looking out the window and straining up, down, left and right, but nothing stood out. Thinking hard, she tried to remember the nearest forest to her home, but that was several hours away. Surely, she had not been taken that far from home?

She looked into the closet to see nothing but blankets and pillows and some hanging clothes. She pushed her hands under them and behind them to find nothing. On the floor of the closet was a flashlight and a first aid kit. Looking through the kit, she couldn't find anything that might help her. She held the flashlight in her hand wondering if she could use that as a weapon. It was better than nothing. She took it out of the closet and set it on the nightstand where she could access it quickly but behind the lamp where it wouldn't be too noticeable to her abductor.

Through the other door was a bathroom that seemed to have a full bathtub and shower. Ranalla rummaged in the drawers of the vanity and under the sink. She couldn't even find cleaning solutions. There were towels and wash cloths along with soap and a toothbrush and toothpaste. There was no nail file or anything she could use as a weapon. Behind the door, she found a robe. Even searching in the shower offered her no tools.

Back in the bedroom, she looked around but nothing aside from the bedside lamp looked like something she could use. Mentally, she noted where it was, where the books were so she could use them if she had to, and everything else that wasn't nailed down. She was not hesitant to use any or all of it to get away.

Another examination of the windows showed that slamming something through it wouldn't work as it was set in small panes with steel frames. She didn't know if she'd have the strength to do it without getting caught. She was determined to use whatever she found.

Frustrated, she flung herself back on the bed almost forgetting the tray that still sat on it. A small piece of a chip flew in the air and landed on her nose. She huffed as she flicked it aside. She had to get a look outside the room but wasn't quite willing to risk trying that yet. She had to get a better feel about her captor. He would find out quickly that she was not a docile captive. She would fight to the death.

Ranalla dug in the nightstand drawer and found a deck of cards and a box of tissue. A good game of solitaire always calmed her down and helped her to think. She was into her tenth game while sitting cross-legged on the bed when she heard someone on the other side of the door. It was a slight noise, but it was someone moving by the door she was sure of. She had no idea if the man was her only captor or if there were scores of others. Ranalla paused with her hand in the air as it was making its way down to place a four of spades on a five of diamonds.

The door opened, and the same man who brought her the food walked in. Without giving her anything but a brief glance, he walked to the closet and opened the door. He pulled the clothes she had seen when she looked through it earlier and returned to the bed. He tossed them beside her. "There are some underclothes in the drawer of the dresser. Get dressed." He turned and walked out without another word.

She looked over at the clothes and back at the door. The mysterious actions of her kidnapper confused her immensely. Where were the screaming, the ropes to tie her up, and the guns to threaten her? None of this was making any sense.

She walked over to the dresser and found a drawer full of women's under-wear. Pulling them out, she noticed they were all her exact size. She quickly pulled on the jeans and t-shirt that were, once again, the perfect size. A pair of new tennis shoes and a pair of socks were next to the dresser. It wasn't long before she was dressed.

It was as though he knew exactly what she was doing. As the last shoe lace was tied, the door opened. He stood in the doorway and simply stared. After a few pregnant moments he turned away and walked off leaving the door open. She assumed it was permission to leave the room. If it wasn't, then she was about to get into a boat load of trouble.

She tentatively walked out of the room. The hallway was dark with a light farther down where Ranalla assumed the man had gone. Her eyes darted around to see other doors, but none of them were open or showed signs of being used.

Each door she passed gave her pause as she expected someone to jump out at her. She had no idea if there were any other people in the house or outside. She was literally and figuratively in the dark. After the third door, she found herself at the end of the hall facing a well-lit living room.

She was right in her assessment of her prison being a cabin, but it was not just any old cabin. This was one done up in style. The wood was in pristine condition. Over the massive stone fireplace was a large flat screen. Her quick glance caught a large couch and several chairs situated around the room.

She sought for an escape. A door to her right appeared to lead out of the building, but there were multiple locks on it. Beside it was a window, as well as two on the opposite wall, where her captor stood looking outside. At least for now, those were not viable. In his hand was a glass he was drinking from.

Without looking at her he spoke. "There is no way out."

She stared at him in shock that he knew exactly what she was thinking. He kept his eyes trained out the window, but for some reason she knew he was watching her every move. Nothing appeared to escape his notice.

He took another long drink from the glass before turning to her. "You can try, but I can guarantee you that you won't be able to." His face possessed no expressions.

Her heart raced. She didn't care what he said; she would find a way out. So far, he appeared to know a lot about her. Surely, he knew she could be stubborn. She raised her chin and stared back at him with narrowed eyes.

He chuckled at her defiant look.

"Why am I here?" There was an angry edge to her voice.

Another sip of his drink. "Too keep you safe." His eyes held hers, their darkness piercing her.

Her stomach quivered from the look. "Safe? You call kidnapping me safe?" Her voice rose with each word. She began to shake with anger. The fear was subsiding. Rage was flowing within.

This time he laughed out loud. His eyes crinkled at the corners. He actually looked younger and more attractive when he laughed. Ranalla mentally shook herself. This was the man who ripped her from her bed in the middle of the night. How could she possibly be attracted to him? She only wanted to get away from him.

"I don't see what's so funny." She crossed her arms in front her. She had an intense desire to scratch his eyes out.

"Safe. What one person sees as safe can have an entirely different meaning to another one." His mouth pulled up on one side with his unique knowledge of the situation. She shook her head in confusion. "What?"

He looked her up and down slowly. "Trust me. You're safer here."

"No. I was safer back in my own place."

He shook his head. "No. You were not." He turned around and walked to the large leather couch. He lowered his tall frame on it. Turning around slightly, he motioned for her to come sit down. "Come on. We have plenty of movies here we can watch."

Her mouth fell open as she stared at him incredulously. He turned around with another chuckle and picked up the remote promptly ignoring her. As the screen flickered to life, she shook her head. His humor regarding this situation was getting on her last nerve. He was succeeding in eliminating her fear. She was beyond angry now.

Tossing her hair back, she looked around and saw a door behind her left shoulder. The kitchen might have something to help her. She quickly made her way in there and began pulling open drawers. She hoped to find something to help her before he made it in there. The first one she pulled on didn't budge. She moved to the next one and then the next one. She slammed her hand on the counter top in frustration.

"You won't find anything to help you in here." His voice startled her. With a squeak, she turned around to find him leaning against the door frame as he watched her with an amused look. Her fingers flexed and longed to rid him of the smile.

"Why?" She leaned against the counter and glared back at him.

"I locked the drawers. You can't access any knives or other sharp objects."

As he spoke, he moved forward like a tiger eyeing his prey.

She quickly looked around for a way out. To her right was a back door. Taking a chance, she ran to it and twisted the knob. Nothing. She tugged on it. The door would not move. She froze when she heard him step right behind her. Ranalla swung around and pressed her back against the door as he moved in closer.

His six foot three frame dwarfed her five foot five body. The slight smile was still on his face as he reached a hand out to lightly touch her hair. He let the golden strands flow through his fingers. He moved to her cheek and caressed it. She pulled back as far as she could. The door knob dug into her lower back.

"You have nothing to fear from me," he whispered. His voice had a sexy edge to it that she noticed, but fear was mingling with the anger now. She just wanted out of there and back home. She wanted to get away from him.

"I beg to differ." Her voice whispered. He was so close to her face. She breathed in his masculine scent.

He gave her cheek one last caress before turning around and leaving her stunned. "Grab a drink out of the fridge and come on in. I found a good comedy."

She looked at the fridge and back to his retreating form. This couldn't be real. Aside from being kidnapped everything seemed so....normal. Just grab a drink. Watch a movie. But she can't have a knife. Had she fallen down the preverbal rabbit hole?

She was thirsty. Opening the fridge, she found an ample supply of drinks from bottled waters to sodas to fruit juice. She pulled out a can of white soda and continued looking over the contents. It was stocked well enough to feed an army, especially as she noticed it was an extra-large refrigerator.

She sighed as she closed the door and leaned against it. Ranalla opened the can and looked into the living room. There he was sitting and waiting on her. What kind of man kidnaps a woman and then acts like this?

Chapter 5

The casualness of the kidnapper confused Ranalla. His actions were not like those of an abductor. She didn't have a lot of experience in that area, but even what she did know did not mesh with the actions of this one. She shook her head as she slowly walked into the living room. He had turned the television on and was surfing channels.

She paused behind the couch and stared at his head of thick black hair. Another glance moved from door to windows. Her exits were pretty well blocked for now. She could either try to watch a movie or hide in her room and go stir crazy. Watching television would give her more time to evaluate the room and even her kidnapper. She shrugged her shoulders and resigned herself to a movie.

Moving around the end of the couch, she settled herself down on the leather sofa in the corner farthest from him. Her eyes stayed on him and watched for any sudden moves. She had the soda can ready to use as a weapon. A smile played around his lips. She had the feeling he had known every move she had made since he left her standing against the door. Pursing her lips she looked at the television screen while keeping an eye on him in her peripheral vision. Her fingers flexed around the aluminum can.

"I won't bite." His low voice floated over to her.

She lowered her eyes but refused to look directly at him. "This coming from the man who kidnapped me and...and..." She turned quickly toward him. "You drugged me. Think I'll trust you now?"

He spared her a quick glance before returning to the movie he started "I only said I wouldn't bite."

His humor unnerved her. This was just too bizarre. She looked back at the screen but couldn't get into the movie. Her body tense, she turned to face him. She didn't trust him at all. All he had to do was make one move, the soda would be in his face, and she'd find something else to hit him with.

Thirty minutes went by. The only time he moved was when he laughed at the comedy scenes. Ranalla had not moved herself as she waited for him to make a move. Without taking his eyes off the movie, he commented, "Enjoying the view?"

Her breath caught in her chest. "What?"

His eyes crinkled from the humor he saw in the situation. "You've sat there the whole time looking at me." He turned to face her. Their eyes met. Hers confused. His amused. "Enjoying it?"

"I....I..Wh...I.." Unable to utter a coherent thought, she jerked around to watch the movie. "Jerk."

His only response was a laugh.

The rest of the movie went by in a blur for Ranalla. Her eyes were focused on the screen, but her attention was on the man beside her. He had her all confused and wound up. What would happen if she dropped her guard? Was that what he wanted her to do so he could pounce on her and finish what he wanted to do to her? And what was that? Why was she there? Money? Rape?

As the credits rolled up, he took the remote to change to what appeared to be satellite feed. He laid the remote between them. She felt his eyes on her. For several moments she refused to look at him but the silence drove her crazy. With pinched lips, she turned to face him and stared back.

"What?"

"Here's the remote. You can choose whatever you want to watch or you can help with dinner."

It was then she noticed how dark it had grown through the windows. The day had zoomed by while he watched the movie and she watched him. Thinking about it quickly, she leaned toward helping with dinner. Surely the drawers would open up to get their food ready. That could be her chance.

She bit her lip and nodded. "I'll help with dinner." Ranalla tried to keep her voice tight. The last thing she wanted was for him to get wind of her true intentions for helping him.

Another smiled appeared on his face. How she wished she could forcefully remove it! "Thought you might choose that." She watched as he stood up and walked into the kitchen leaving her to follow.

She must be going crazy. None of this made sense. Hearing a drawer open, she got up and entered the brightly lit kitchen. She hadn't noticed before how beautiful it was. The large island in the center was perfect for cooking a huge meal. Everything was rustic as the rest of the cabin, but in an elegant manner with stainless steel appliances and granite tops. This was no hunting cabin. This was luxury. Again, nothing made sense.

He was pulling out various items from the fridge. She looked around for which drawer was open, but all were closed. One was unlocked. It had to be, but which one? She walked up to the island, leaned against it, and hoped the casual stance belied her true action of investigating each drawer within sight.

Her attention was pulled in the direction of the food. Her heart sank as she saw ground beef, precut lettuce, hamburger buns, sliced cheese, and mayo. Even the mushrooms were already sliced. There was no need for a knife.

In his apparently typical act of not looking at her, he commented, "You'll notice that I usually plan ahead."

She huffed and crossed her arms in front of her. This was going to be harder than she thought. If she believed in such things, she'd believe he was a mind reader.

"What can I do to help?"

"There are packages of seasoning I've pulled out on the counter by the fridge. Season the meat and form patties." He took the mushrooms and began sautéing them in a small skillet. She frowned at the stuff he had managed to pull out before she got in there. It was as though it had been done by magic.

"I need a bowl."

He picked up one from in front of him and handed it to her. His eyes met hers, and he said, "Told you I'm always prepared."

Eyes narrowed, she jerked the bowl out of his hand and began opening the package of meat. Between the two of them, it didn't take long to get the meal ready. Her mouth began to water as the delicious smell of burgers filled the kitchen. This was her favorite burger with mushrooms in a steak sauce to complement the meat and cheese.

Once they were all done, she grabbed their drinks and followed him to the table that was in the corner by the living room door. As she sat the drinks down, he appeared with a bag of chips. She looked around in surprise. She had not heard any door open or close.

Refusing to give him another chance to laugh at her, she sat down and avoided his gaze. Instead, she focused on her food. It took all she had to control her facial expressions.

She almost groaned with satisfaction as she bit into the succulent burger. It was one of the best she had ever had. It was perfect to her taste in every way. The meat was medium rare, the mushrooms were tender, and the cheese was Baby Swiss. It was as though he knew her likes. She paused before the second bite. As the thought flitted into her mind, she pushed it aside. It couldn't be true. No way. How could he know those details of her life?

Chapter 6

S he noticed that it was getting dark out as she took the last bite of her burger. This would be her first night as a captive. A whole day had slid by. She had no idea what it would hold or what tomorrow would hold. Plus, too many things were tugging at the edges of her brain. Things were not adding up right. If she could only focus, she might be able to figure out what called to her.

She sat back in her chair and glanced over at the man who mystified her. He was munching on the last of his chips. His casual and relaxed demeanor threw her into further confusion.

"Now what?" She crossed her arms around her. She wanted to scream at him.

His eyes met hers before looking back down at the table. "We clean up." His tone questioned her intent behind her own question.

"I know that. Afterwards." Exasperation filled her voice.

He picked up the plates as he stood up and walked toward the sink. "Don't know what you mean."

She grabbed the bag of chips and tossed them on the island as she stood up and faced him. He looked at the bag and then at her. His eyebrows arched as he looked at her. "Careful. We'll only have crumbs if you keep that up." He turned back to the sink and began running water for the dishes.

Angrily, she picked up the bag and dropped them on the counter again , deliberately letting them fall from several inches above the counter. He looked back at her without blinking. Huffing, she slammed her fists on the bag. "There! Now you have crumbs." Her chest rose with the heavy breathing caused by her anger.

He continued getting the water ready to wash the dishes. He was the strangest kidnapper. He ignored her. He did not wave a gun at her or hurt her or tie her up. He simply ignored her.

"Why are you ignoring me?" She was beside herself at his actions. It was all so confusing.

He put the plates in the soapy hot water and began washing them . "I'm not ignoring you."

"What do you call this?" She flung her hands out at him.

"Enjoying myself." A smile could be heard in his voice, though all she saw was the back of his head.

Ranalla felt her heart begin to race as the anger inside her boiled. She gave in to the urge to hit him. She looked around and found the skillet the hamburgers were fried in still sitting on the stove waiting to be cleaned. She quickly glanced at her captor. He was focused on running the water. Quietly she moved to the stove. She picked it up, intent on hitting him over the head with it. As she grasped the handle, she felt arms sweep around her and wet hands close over hers. His body was pressed against hers tightly. She closed her eyes knowing she was now caught.

Against her ear, she felt his warm breath as he whispered. "Let go." She was acutely aware of every part of him. Now, he would become more physical. He had to. She had, after all, tried to kill him .

She gripped the handle tighter. His hands tightened in response.

"Let go. You can't win this, Ranalla." He didn't move. Just held her still.

Her body stiffened in defiance. She knew she wasn't strong enough to fight him. That's why she reached for the skillet as a weapon. It would have done what she couldn't do on her own against his larger and more powerful frame. Now, her only weapon was to be taken from her. Slowly, she loosened her grip. Feeling it, he gradually pulled her hands from the skillet. In case she tried to reach for it again, his hands held firmly onto her.

When the skillet was a few inches away, she felt him take a deep breath. Then he quickly turned her around and pinned her arms behind her. In doing so, he forced her body into full contact with his. Her eyes shot up to glare at him.

The man lowered his face to hers till there was just a hair's breadth between their noses. The amusement in his eyes vanished. Cold, hard, eyes now bore into hers.

"Never do that again. I don't want to have to lock you in your room." His voice was full of promise.

Her breathing was rapid as she nodded her head and swallowed. This was the first move he had made that was like what she expected from a kidnapper, and it terrified her. Anger had been replaced with fear of what was to come.

He held her for an extra few seconds before releasing her hands. Unsure of what he was doing, she didn't move at first. Sensing he was letting her go, she stepped back. She stopped quickly when his hand shot out to stop her.

With the other he grabbed the skillet and put it in the sink. He turned to the sink and said, "Go to your room."

Without another word, she left. Now she was afraid.

She was shaking when she walked into the bedroom. Closing the door, she sagged against it. Her hand came to her throat. What would happen now that she had caused him to act like the kidnapper he was?

She paced back and forth across the bedroom floor. According to the clock, ten minutes went by. Ten more. She stopped pacing when it announced it had been half an hour. What was he doing? Should she venture out? This was something she hoped to avoid during her lifetime.

She stopped before the closed door and hit her hands against her legs. No longer able to take it, she had to know what was happening. Tentatively, she tried the doorknob and found that it turned. She wasn't locked in, after all.

She opened it only a crack and peered down the dark hallway. The living room was full of light. She bit her lower lip and forced herself down the hallway for the second time that day. Again she paused in the door of the living room. He was sitting on the couch where he was during the movie. On the screen, a documentary on books played. He was acting like nothing had happened.

Her arms crossed in front of her, and she realized that she was scared. She had angered him and was now at his mercy. Unsure if she should walk into the living room or not, she swallowed hard and thought of her options. She could just go back to her room. Her decision made, she pulled back ready to do just that when he spoke.

"Don't just stand there. Come on in. I've got some popcorn here for you." He never even looked at her.

Ranalla set her shoulders back and walked forward. At the edge of the couch, she stopped. For some ludicrous reason, a part of her wanted to apologize to him. She nervously rubbed her hands down her jeans. It made it all worse that he wouldn't look at her. She felt like a spurned child.

"I...."She breathed in deep. "I wa...."

At that moment he looked up and all thoughts fled from her mind. She could have sworn he had a look of tenderness in his eyes. It was not what she had expected.

"Sit," he said softly.

She slid to the couch as he watched. Once seated, he turned back to the show. In front of her on the coffee table was a bowl of popcorn and a cold glass of juice. The ice was still fresh. How did he do that? It's as though he knew exactly when she was coming out.

They watched the show in silence. At the first commercial, he reached for the popcorn bowl and set it between them with a slight smile. Ranalla tried to smile back. Everything was so odd. Here she was sharing a bowl of popcorn with her abductor. Yep, she needed psychological help.

Chapter 7

The show ended just as Ranalla finished her juice. She set it down on the coffee table and glanced over at the stranger next to her.

"I don't know your name." She waited for him to say that he couldn't tell her. If he told her, that meant he planned on killing her. Everything hung on his answer.

His eyes met hers. For a few moments, he said nothing. The air between them was pregnant with fear and uncertainty. In a half smile, he said, "Vince. My name is Vince."

She stopped breathing for a minute as her heart pushed into her throat. Death it was to be then. "Is that your real name or something you're just saying to me?"

He concentrated intensely on running his finger around the rim of his glass. Taking her by surprise, he looked up. "Vincent de Marte. That's my real name." He watched her face closely.

Ranalla squeezed her eyes tight. "So, that means you're going to kill me." Her eyes shot open when he laughed.

Vince was shaking his head. "No. No, I'm not going to kill you." He stood up and took the popcorn bowl into the kitchen.

She jumped up and ran after him. "Why not?"

He turned around with an incredulous look on his face. "You want to die? You wanted to get away so bad earlier that you tried to bash my head with a skillet! Now, you're upset because I'm not going to kill you?"

"You told me your name. How can you let me go if I know your name?" She stopped a few feet away from him in case he decided to go ahead and get it over with.

His face became serious. He walked toward her and pushed her backwards until her posterior was against the island. He looked over her face and tried to read what was going through her mind. "I'm the reason you won't die. Keep that in mind. I don't want you to die."

Abruptly he turned to put up the bowl and his glass. He leaned his arms against the sink and hung his head. "Go on to bed. You've had a long and stressful day."

Unsure of what to do, she stared at his bent back. She closed her eyes against the confusing thoughts racing through her head. Maybe it would be safer just to go back to the room and find some peace. She turned and retreated down the hall.

He listened to her footsteps fade and the sound of the door click. This was not how he wanted things to be. She deserved more than a life on the run, but that is what she was faced with. Her life hung in the balance, and he was determined to make sure it didn't fall into an abyss.

Chapter 8

As Ranalla showered, the streams of water hitting her body felt so good that her mind began to clear. Here she was in the middle of nowhere with some man named Vincent de Marte. Not only did he lock all the windows and doors but also the kitchen cabinets. And during all of this, she ate popcorn with him while they watched a movie. Maybe the shower was not doing such a good job after all.

When she had escaped into her room, she had paced the length of it several times before stopping to sniff the air. It was then she realized that it had been almost two days since she last showered. Maybe that would help her think more clearly.

Once her shoulder length hair was rinsed, she got out of the shower and used the robe on the back of the door. She found a hairbrush in one of the drawers. It didn't take her long to brush her wet hair. She walked into the bedroom and looked in the dresser for something to sleep in. What she found was not anything she would have felt comfortable in. Every piece was in her size, but it was all satin and lace. She preferred shorts and tank tops.

Pulling open a lower drawer, she found exactly what she was looking for. A short time later, finally comfortable in a pair of black short shorts and a maroon t-shirt, she slid into the bed.

As she reached to turn the bedside light off, the door opened. She sat up staring at Vince as he walked in closing the door behind him. Without looking at her, he began unbuttoning his shirt.

"Whoa! What are you doing?" She scrambled up against the headboard and pulled the sheet with her. Her eyes were wide. No murder, but rape. That was his plan. She had let her guard down so he had the advantage.

He stopped halfway through unbuttoning his shirt. "I'm getting ready for bed."

"In here?" Her voice squeaked.

"I'm not sleeping on the couch if that is what you meant." He rolled his eyes and finished unbuttoning.

"I'll sleep there." She jumped out of the bed and grabbed a pillow to take with her.

Her way was blocked by his hand on the closed door. Terror rose up within her. She was fully aware of his now naked chest. She tried not to look at it. Instead she focused on the muscular arm blocking her. Not much of a better idea.

"Get back in bed, Ranalla. Your virtue is safe." His voice sounded weary.

She turned to look at him. A part of her ached for him, a part she was desperately beating down and putting it back in its place.

"Why here? There are other rooms."

"Those are locked and have no beds in them. This is the only bed and I'm too tired to look for anything else right now."

She eyed him warily.

"I promise I won't touch you without your permission."

He seemed sincere. With a short nod, she pulled back and made her way to the far side of the bed. It wasn't like she had much of a choice. She crawled back under the covers and moved as close to the edge of the bed as she could without falling off. It was only then that she realized that the flashlight she had put aside as a weapon was on the other side of the bed. To move now was to only draw his attention. He was already too good at guessing her next move.

As she lay rigid, she could hear him getting undressed. Ranalla closed her eyes and tried not to listen to the sounds of his shirt hitting the floor. Mentally she was calculating the steps to the door and what weapons were within reach, the books. When she heard his jeans unzipping, she wanted to bolt out of the room.

The covers shifted and the bed dipped under his weight. She held her breath, and it wasn't until he settled down on his side that she let it out. She heard him reach out and turn off the light throwing the room into total darkness.

She stared into the dark and listened. Not a sound could be heard until his voice reached her.

"Goodnight, Ranalla."

She turned her head just slightly. "Goo...goodnight."

She didn't move. The sound of his breathing evened out. It was only then that she relaxed. Hours later she finally fell asleep. She was too afraid to make a move to escape. He was too close.

Once Ranalla allowed herself to drift off to sleep, she fell into a deep slumber. Her body was tired from tensing and waiting on something to happen. Exhaustion finally won out.

Chapter 9

- -

As she relaxed and burrowed deeper into the warmth, she noticed a change in the texture of the bed. She didn't remember it being this hard. The blankets and sheets she fell asleep under had been soft and inviting. She took a deep breath and stopped cold as she flexed her fingers and realized that it was not a sheet her hand moved over, but a hard, muscular chest. And a bare chest at that.

Awareness shot through her. Even without opening her eyes, she could see what was happening. He was lying on his back. She was pressed up against his side with one of his arms firmly holding her waist. There was not even enough room left for air to pass between them.

She was afraid to breathe in case it woke him up. She could feel his regular breathing telling her he was still out. If she was careful, she could move to her side of the bed without waking him up. It was the arm around her waist that could prove difficult. Thinking over her options, she could not see any other path. Ranalla was about to shift away when she paid closer attention to the hand that lay on her hip. She could have sworn it moved slightly.

Seconds that seemed like hours passed as she lay still before she felt it again. His fingers moved. It wasn't a sleep-induced twitch. The fingers actually moved in an almost imperceptible action. They gradually began to move in a more deliberate and noticeable caress. The path of the fingers grew wider with each stoke.

The act was up. She couldn't pretend anymore. Not moving was going to drive her crazy and give him the wrong message. "You can let me go now." Her voice was thick from sleep yet sharp with anger.

His fingers did not stop. They increased in pressure while staying in one place. She felt a low rumble of laughter within his chest. She tried not to think of the feel of his hot skin under her cheek or how good his body felt against hers. Her heart began to race. A roar filled her ears. Even lying down, she began to feel light headed. She wanted to scream.

"I'm rather enjoying this." His chest rumbled beneath her again. The feelings hitting her like a freight train were more than she could handle at the moment. Anger at his smugness threatened to overcome her. There was an attraction that caused her to mentally go into a tailspin as it collided with the rage boiling up within her.

She used the hand on his chest to push up and away. He allowed her to do so but kept her within his arm. His eyes were closed as he lay back on the white sheets. He appeared so dark and dangerous laying there.

"Let me go," she repeated through gritted teeth. She was fully aware of his body against hers and her hand pressed firmly on his chest. She knew he was muscular, but the extent of it surprised her.

One eye opened to look directly at her. "Why?"

She strained back. "This is not right."

The eye closed back. "Maybe you shouldn't have come over and snuggled up to me."

"Wha....I never....I did not!" Her shoulders rose in indignation. All struggles stopped as she took in his words.

"I was laying here and the next thing I knew you were putting your arm around me and pressing your body against mine."

She began to sputter again in anger. He didn't hold back his laughter as his arm freed her. Taking advantage of it, she scooted to her side of the bed and quickly jumped out. Grabbing her clothes from the previous day, she ran into the bathroom and slammed the door. His laughter followed her.

She dropped her clothes on the counter top and leaned her arms on the sink. Looking in the mirror, she tried to find reason in all this. Some sense of .....sensibility. Nothing. All she saw was a highly embarrassed woman who had for the first time woken up in the arms of a man. Her kidnapper of all people!

Her face flushed more at the memory of how it felt to be so intimately close to him. She brought her hand up and stared at it. His flesh under that hand was so...... She couldn't even come up with a word that would describe correctly the heat form his skin. He was firm and perfectly sculptured. The skin....Ranalla cursed under her breath as the memories flooded back.

Ranalla turned on the cold water and splashed her face with it. The sudden coldness calmed her racing heart. Looking back into the mirror, she glared at herself.

"What is going on? I'm kidnapped but I feel like it is .... It doesn't feel like a kidnapping." Slamming her hand on the counter, she quickly got dressed and took a deep breath before walking out to face him.

Just a few feet into the room, she stopped cold. The bed was empty. His clothes were gone. Once again, he was a step ahead of her.

Chapter 10

Ranalla found him, dressed in jeans and a black button up shirt, in the kitchen and cooking breakfast as he whistled. The smell of bacon stopped her cold. Her mouth was open and ready to yell at him, but all she could do was take a deep breath of the seductive smell of the bacon.

"Got your favorite bacon and scrambled eggs with mushrooms and Havarti cheese." He began filling up two plates on the island.

A smile spread across her face as she watched the eggs slide down onto the plate next to the bacon. It took a few moments for his words to sink in. Favorite? How would he know her favorite breakfast food?

"Wait." She pulled her eyes from the food and stared at him. The smile was long gone now.

He must have known he had said something wrong because his own smile faded as he picked up the plates and took them to the table. She turned toward him. "Favorite? How do you know this is my favorite?"

He ignored her like a child caught with his hand in the cookie jar. Motioning toward the other chair, he said, "Come on. It's getting cold."

Her mouth fell open. "Don't avoid the question. How did you know this is my favorite breakfast?" Each word came out like a bullet.

He sat down the fork he had in hand and stared at the plate before him. Sighing deeply, he turned toward her. "Okay. I know a lot about you. Now, let's eat."

She rushed forward and grabbed his arm as he began to turn back to the food. He closed his eyes and waited. "No. Explain. Now."

This time he stood up and faced her. "What did you expect? I kidnapped you. I had to know everything about you. Satisfied?"

"No. Honestly, I'm not. Would you be? Think about it. None of this makes sense to me. Not one thing makes sense. Why take me? You haven't killed me. You haven't hurt me. Why? Oh..." Her mouthed formed an O. "Ransom. You're waiting on my father to pay for me?"

The thought had never crossed her mind. It had been five years since she had last spoken to her father, and it was a memory she would rather have forgotten. But he was wealthy. He was well-known and she wouldn't be surprised if he had been involved in more than his share of shady deals.

He glanced away for a second. "Ransom? No. I told you. I brought you to safety."

"From what? Safe from what?"

"Ranalla..." He ran his hands through his hair. "A contract was put out on you."

She blinked. "A contract? You mean like the hire to kill kind of contract?"

He nodded. "If I had left you in your bed night before last, you'd be dead right now."

"Dead?" She just began parroting everything he said. He saw her face turn white and her eyes begin to take a distant look to them. Taking her by her shoulders, he directed her to the other chair. She sat down without realizing what she was doing. She allowed him to direct her. "Someone wants me dead?"

He squatted down on his heels where he could be eye level with her. "Ranalla, it's going to be fine. I got you out in time."

She pulled herself back to him though she still had a dazed look. "Why? Why did you save me?"

A slight smile pulled at his lips. "Why not? I don't like to see innocent people die."

"How did you know about it?" She asked the one question he wished she had just let left alone.

"I overhead it. Let's leave it at that for now, okay."

She looked hard into his eyes. "Are you telling me the truth? This isn't a trick to make me cooperative?"

This time he laughed. "No. Not a trick. I promise. Plus, I don't see you actually being cooperative."

His eyes were so deep and honest to her. She couldn't see any deception in their depths. Her gut told her to trust him. He might be the only thing standing between her and death.

In response, she nodded and saw the relief in his eyes.

"Now, let me reheat all this since you let it get cold." He stood up and picked up their plates.

She gave a nervous laugh. "Sorry." Everything was still sinking in. The shock of his words made it all seem much more unreal.

They ate their meal in quiet, but Ranalla could feel a peace between them that wasn't there before. In a way, she was more confused than ever. Now their relationship had completely changed. She was still leery of him. There was something dangerous, yet attractive about him. Was what he said the truth? Could she really trust him?

After they had cleaned up, they sat on the couch and watched another movie. Or at least she pretended to watch it. The thought of her father earlier had dredged up a lot of memories, most of which she would have preferred to have stayed buried.

Five years ago, she had stormed out of her father's house slamming a door on her past and her name. She had abandoned Ranalla White that night and became Ranalla Johnson, taking her mother's maiden name. It had not been pretty, what led up to the change. The fight began when she came in at a few minutes after three in the morning.

Her high heel shoes were dangling from her hands as she tried to quietly close the door. The marble floor was ice cold on her feet. She turned around thinking it was a success only to find her father standing on the stairs of his mansion glaring at her. His silk dress robe did not take away from his aura of power and his look of disapproval.

The all too familiar disdain on his face slammed into her. No matter how many times those silver eyes beneath the bushy eyebrows looked at her with disgust, it never quit hurting. A father should be loving and approving, not one that looked at their only child as if she were excrement from dirty farm animals.

Many thought him handsome, but Ranalla knew what lurked beneath the façade. She knew the black evil that attempted to stay hidden behind the face of generosity and politeness. Once those not part of the inner circle left his presence, the smiling sculpted mask would change to be replaced by a face that Ranalla came to believe the incarnation of the devil himself.

"You're home early." His deep voice echoed in the vacant entrance way that was larger than the home of the average person.

Realizing there was no more sense in trying to be quiet, she walked up to the stairs and looked at her father who had deliberately stayed ten steps up to emphasize his power over her. What he didn't realize was that his power was just a glimmer compared to its strength just twenty-four hours earlier.

"I'd have been home earlier if I could have caught a taxi before I walked fifteen blocks." She glared up at the man who had become her enemy.

He frowned. She had once thought him handsome with his thick white hair and dignified jaw line. Most women took a double or triple-take when he walked by. His presence demanded attention. She never saw him as a role model or loving parent, but she understood women's reactions to him - until now. All she saw as she looked up at him now was the scaly serpent that resided under the well-developed exterior.

"Walked? Why didn't Sheldon bring you home?"

She smiled sweetly letting honey fall from every word. "Because the man you have so dearly set your heart on as your future son-in-law, refused to bring me home."

The frown deepened. "Why not? What did you do?"

She raised her eyebrows in surprise. "What did I do? Actually, I refused to be raped. That's all."

"Raped? I doubt it. Just say it like it is. You teased him and then refused to follow through." He looked down at her with disappointment. "Shame on you for torturing the poor boy."

Her calm demeanor fled at those words. "Shame on me! Shame on me? That's what my father says because I refused to give up my virginity?"

"Ranalla Anne, you know that I want Sheldon as part of this family. If he wants to get between your legs, so be it. It's one step closer to him being where I want him."

Her breathing increased. She had to keep telling herself not to hyperventilate. She couldn't believe what she was hearing. "So you'd trade my virtue for a business merger?"

"What else are you good for?" The words slammed into her like ice water.

"Loving words to your only child."

"A disappointing child who doesn't know her role. It would have been better if your mother had aborted you like I told her to."

She turned around and walked back to the large gilded front door she had just tiptoed through. Her hand was on the knob when he spoke loudly. "Where do you think you are going?"

She looked over her shoulder at him. "Aborting myself from your life." Silently sneaking in, she left with a slam that echoed into the deepest parts of the empty mansion.

Chapter 11

With the new unspoken truth between them, Vince let up and agreed to take Ranalla outside. He watched her face for any signs of deception as she asked for this privilege. Satisfied with what he saw, he agreed to it.

The warm sunshine felt so good on Ranalla's skin. She had only been locked up for one day, but it felt like years. When denied something, the body craves it more than anything.

Stepping out on the small back porch, Ranalla felt liberated. Still in essence a prisoner, it felt good to be outside the four walls. Vince stayed close as she walked from the house. It was slow going, but she thoroughly enjoyed the scents and sounds around her.

A slight breeze danced over her bare arms. She shivered slightly at the coolness of it, and chill bumps rose up on her skin until she stepped further into the sunlight and felt the warmth of the sun. Birds were twittering in the air. She could see hints of spring courting in the air as a blue bird flew past her with another one not far behind. A movement out of the corner of her eye brought a small rabbit into view. She smiled as it froze and watched them intently. Once it decided they were safe, it resumed munching the fresh grass growth.

Looking around, she noticed that the cabin was deep in the woods as she had suspected. Trees were thick and getting thicker with the spring growth. The cabin sat in a small clearing and was the only place she saw the sun able to penetrate to the ground completely.

She raised her face up to the sun's rays and drank in the warmth. Opening her eyes, she saw Vince leaning against a tree watching her. Instead of the eyes of a kidnapper, he was watching her with a much more intimate look. Her heart skipped a beat.

After his announcement of a hit on her, Ranalla had a lot of thinking to do. She used the excuse of having to use the bathroom to get some time alone to think. He was her kidnapper, but now it was conceivable he was there to protect her. After all, she was the daughter of the shipping tycoon that did more than just shipping. Many people feared and hated her father. There had been several attempts on her life before, but that happened when she was much younger. It stopped as she got older and the protection detail became tougher. It also stopped when it became apparent that her father was not one that would pay anything for his daughter. Once she became a teenager, he did not hide from the world the fact he could not stand the sight of his only child.

But that didn't stop it completely. She had heard of botched attempts to kidnap her for ransom. Usually she dismissed them as just rumors, but now she had a different perspective on them. It made sense having Vince as saving her, but his methodology was a little strange. Then again, she would never have gone with him willingly.

Once she had accepted him as a protector instead of a kidnapper, she felt a complete change between them. She had ignored the electricity she felt before with him as the bad guy. Now she didn't try to push those feelings away quite as hard. He wasn't such a bad guy after all.

Ranalla didn't want to leave the sun. The warmth felt good as did the fresh air. Lowering herself to the ground, she sat cross-legged and played with the grass between her fingers. It felt nice as she ran her fingers over the new sprouts. She sensed his presence before she saw his shadow. Without looking up at him, she said, "Thank you."

Vince lowered himself down beside her with one knee up to rest his arm on. "You're welcome." He plucked a blade of grass and toyed with it. "I don't want you to have to feel like a prisoner."

She looked at him. "But I still am, right?"

"I'm only trying to protect you." He sounded sincere. She wanted to believe him; she needed to believe him.

Ranalla looked at him. "I think I realize that." She let out a short laugh. "I was thinking of the last time anyone tried to protect me. I can't remember it ever happening after Mother died."

His eyes shot up looking at her intently. He searched her face for emotion. "That long?" She detected a little surprise in his voice.

She nodded. "Yeah. She took the brunt of Father's anger. Her death in the car accident took away the only shield I had from his disappointment in me." Tears threatened to pool in her eyes.

"What does he say to you now? You don't live the life of the daughter of Gregory Stipold." He knew most of the answers but wanted to hear them from her. There was always more than one side to a story.

She looked down at the grass and pushed it around under her hand. When she spoke, it came out as a whisper. "I don't like being his daughter. He's disowned me. I left him and his life."

"Why?" He pushed for more.

"He was willing to sell me and my virginity to gain an empire."

Vince stiffened. Her words were blunt and to the point. She raised her eyes and looked beyond him toward the trees without really seeing them.

"It didn't matter that the man he sold me to was abusive. I was looking to get out of it all before any damage happened." She swallowed. "Father wasn't pleased. He would have preferred I allow myself to be beaten and raped as long as he got what he wanted." She took in a deep breath. "He announced that it would have been better if I had never been born. I found out a lot about him in that one instance. I saw him for the snake he was, and I was ashamed to be his daughter so I walked out. I left it all behind."

"Regret it?" His voice was soft.

She shook her head. "No. Not at all. I've loved being able to work and feel like I am worth something. I get more appreciation from those I work with than my own father. And that is fine." She sat back with a smile. "My life has been better in the last five years than it ever was before."

The smile faded as she looked hard at him. "I guess now the question is what am I going to do with my future?"

He looked away. "I hope one where you find a lot more happiness."

She searched his face for answers. "Where do we go from here?"

"We stay here until we can move on." No matter how he answered, it came out cryptic.

"To where?" She pushed, needing to know answers.

"It depends on when the hunt begins." He glanced up at the sky.

Confused, she looked at him. He sighed. "Right now your death is waiting to be confirmed. When it appears that you're alive, they'll begin hunting you."

"Who?" Her heart began to pound.

"The ones who want you dead."

She sighed and glared at him. "I figured that. Who are they?"

"Ones who don't appreciate you or know you." His voice lowered to a soft whisper.

"You're avoiding my questions." The irritation in her voice was not disguised.

"Nope. Just not answering them the way you want." He smiled at her reaction to the evasive responses.

"Are you always this stubborn?"

"You don't know the half of it." His smile widened.

Ranalla couldn't help smile back at him. "Why did you kidnap me? Why didn't you just tell me about the contract?"

His eyebrows shot up in amusement. "Do you really think you would have believed me? Would you have gone with me?"

Nodding, she chuckled. "Good point."

His head shot up as he listened intently. He stood up in a flash and grabbed her arm pulling her with him. With abruptness he pushed her to the cabin. She stumbled as he moved her forward.

"Get in now." His voice now was commanding.

"What?" She looked around and tried to see what he saw. It was only trees and sky.

"Get in!" His hands were rough as he pushed her in and pulled his cell phone out of his pocket. Suddenly she heard the door locks click shut. She spun around as noises from all over the house could be heard. All windows darkened as thick shades came down on them automatically and plunged the house into a blackness that rivaled the deepest caves. The whole house appeared to withdraw into a shell of armor that no light was able to penetrate.

She rubbed her arm where he had grabbed her. His gentleness from before was gone, and she was afraid to move. In the blackness she had no idea where he was or where she was. She knew she was in the kitchen, but was disoriented as to which direction was what. The darkness didn't allow her to see anything at all. Tentatively reaching out with one hand, she felt the edge of the island. Its cool counter felt comforting. Moving closer to it, she felt a little better. There was something familiar.

The silence was deafening. Vince had made no noise. Something told her he was not in the same room as her, but there was no way she could know for sure. It was as though she was completely alone.

Fear enveloped her as at the same time she heard the sound of a helicopter and felt a hand over her mouth. An arm shot around her to keep her from moving. Her heart pounded in her ears. It was only a low voice that penetrated the roar and grabbed her attention.

Chapter 12

Vince's voice was soft against her ear. "Shhh. I'm right here. Don't make a sound." He waited for her to nod before he pulled his hand slowly away from her mouth.

She still couldn't see a thing, but felt his body against her back and one of his arms tightly wrapped around her waist. Her deep, quiet breathing belied the pounding of her heart. She was on alert for any noise that would clue her in to what was happening. The whir of helicopter blades broke the silence and passed on over them, but still they didn't move.

Silence encompassed the cabin and took on a life of its own as it drew from their pounding hearts. Ranalla didn't bat an eye until she felt Vince's arm relax. He still didn't move away from her as though expecting something else. Moments ticked by as they both waited.

"Stay here." He spoke in a whisper as he moved away. His hushed voice boomed in the silence. She wished he would come back. His warmth was gone and she felt vulnerable in the pitch black. A flicker of light appeared in front of her when he pulled out a candle, struck a match, and its small flame sputtered to life.

The small light did not reach past the kitchen island. The darkness was too thick for the flame to penetrate it. The flame lit up Vince who was looking at Ranalla fiercely. Her eyes widened when she saw within the reach of the light a gun in his hand that was pointed up and ready to be used. This was a man trained to kill.

He shook his head as her mouth moved to speak. His body was rigid. His eyes never left hers. Finally his eyes closed, and relief flooded his face as he lowered the gun.

"They're gone."

She spoke in a whisper. "Who?"

He didn't answer. He moved back into the dark out of her sight. She began to panic until he reappeared without the gun and with a more relaxed look about him.

"I thought I'd have a few more days before the search began." He ran his hands through his hair.

She looked up toward the ceiling. "Did they see us?"

"No." He opened up the fridge flooding the room with more light. Ranalla blinked at the sudden brightness pulling her hand up to shield her eyes.

"Could they tell we were in here?" Her words came out fast.

He handed her a cold soda before reaching back in for his own. "No. The shutters helped, and there are heat detection scramblers in the walls and ceilings. There is no way for sure they'd know we were here." He closed the door, and they were enveloped in darkness again except for the small candle's flickering light.

"Who were they?" She popped open the can and took a sip, and the cold liquid helped to give her a sense of reality.

"Your executioners." He moved away again. "Close your eyes." She barely got them closed before the lights came on. She blinked several times trying to adjust to the temporary blinding light. Vince seemed unaffected as he moved about blowing out the candle and getting back in the fridge.

"Let's have a sandwich." He pulled out all the fixings before he noticed she had not moved.

Her face was bland as she watched him. He stopped moving and walked toward her. His eyes softened when he saw just how scared she was. He placed both hands on her face and held her.

"It's okay," he reassured her.

Her eyes searched his. "How can you act so calm?"

"Too many years of practice. We've bought ourselves more time. That's all we need." His thumb caressed her cheek.

She should have pulled back at the intimate touch, but she was too numb and confused. It was so surreal and it was her reality at the moment. "I don't think I could get used to it."

He chuckled as he turned back to their food. "Hopefully you won't have to. Now, let's have a sandwich and watch a movie."

They spent the rest of the day inside watching movies. Ranalla was grateful she had the chance to go out into the sunshine earlier. She had a gut feeling that it would be a while before she could do it again.

Vince appeared to be enjoying the movie, but Ranalla could not concentrate. The fear felt in the kitchen earlier as the helicopter passed over consumed her thoughts.

The blinds were kept down. She was beginning to feel more of a prisoner than she had been before. Noticing her restlessness, he turned to her. "What kind of books do you like to read?"

She arched one eyebrow. "You mean you don't know?"

He closed his eyes and chuckled. "Caught me." He stood up. "I'll be right back."

As he left the room she turned on the couch, crouched on her knees, and stared at the doorway in the hall he disappeared through. A moment later he returned with a rather large box. She turned her body in line with his until he stopped in front of the couch. Lowering the box to the coffee table, he smiled.

"Have fun." He stepped back and watched.

She narrowed her eyes at him before cautiously opening the box. When she pulled the second flap back, she saw books. She wasted no time emptying the box. Book after book was pulled out and laid on the table. Each one was on her to-read list on her book club website. She pointed at the books.

"You did stalk me." Her tone was accusing.

"You could say that." He settled down on the couch and began watching another movie.

"Do you know how creepy weird this is?" Her heart raced. A part of her was afraid, but another part was excited.

"You gonna read or keep interrupting my movie?"

She shook her head and laughed softly. She was going crazy. Absolutely crazy. What woman enjoyed the spoils of a stalker?

Chapter 13

She spent the rest of the afternoon losing herself in other worlds. The fear of earlier fled as she forgot reality, devouring page after page of the books. The first one she chose was a lighthearted chick lit that gave her a good laugh. She didn't realize how much time had passed until Vince patted her foot. She was stretched out on the couch lost in the world of a bunch of women dealing with men problems. At his touch, she looked up reluctantly from the pages.

"Dinner. Are you ready to eat?" Amusement danced across his face.

"Wha...? Dinner?" Her thoughts were still on the scene she had just left of one woman who was caught spying on her husband as he was attempting to organize a surprise party for her.

He laughed. "You'd make a good parrot. I'll yell when it's ready."

She nodded absently and returned to the comedy before her.

Vince continued laughing as he disappeared into the kitchen to pull dinner together. The noise from the opening drawers and cabinets didn't even come close to getting her attention. The book had taken her completely away from the cabin and the problems in her life.

The delicious aroma drifted in from the kitchen, distracting her from the book and causing her nose to twitch. Something smelled wonderful. She lowered it and glanced toward the kitchen. Vince was moving around from stove to island whistling softly. Her focus moved from the smell of the food to the man moving about.

She had never considered a man in the kitchen to be sexy. Then again she had never really seen a guy in the kitchen except on television. She knew for sure she was heading for the loony bin. Her kidnapper was causing butterflies in her stomach and making her feel all warm and fuzzy. The longer she watched him, the more she desired him.

Her hands itched to slide all over that muscular body as she remembered that morning when she found herself in his arms. She didn't even know that he had saved her then, and she still enjoyed the feel of his arms around her. Maybe it was because she had such little experience with men. Maybe it was because he was the first man to really treat her with kindness and care.

Ranalla's experience with men was almost nonexistent. As a teenager, her father had shipped her off to a boarding school as far away from him as possible. She spent eight years there and didn't even come home on the holidays. There was always a reason she couldn't come. Now she knew it was because her father didn't want her around. He lived his life as though she did not exist.

When life at boarding school was done, she went straight to college and majored in English literature. The daughter of a multi-millionaire, she had no idea what she wanted to do in her life. Her life would be taken care of for a long time, so she didn't really have to do much of anything.

The all-women's college she attended even shielded her from men. Many of the girls would go into town and meet boys, but Ranalla always felt awkward. She had gone once and regretted it.

They had gone to a local hangout that served alcohol. Ranalla had never seen so much wild activity. The group of five she was with quickly found boys who were also looking for a good time. The one that was paired with her thought he was God's gift to women. Now that she thought about it, he reminded her quite a bit of Sheldon.

This guy with a large, too bright smile kept brushing his blond hair back with his hand even though it had not moved all night. The entire conversation was about him. When it did turn to focus on her, it was to comment on her large chest and tight jeans. Ranalla had never felt more uncomfortable.

As they were leaving the bar, she made to hail a taxi. Her 'date' for the evening tried to forcibly put her in his car while telling her that he was going to get something out of the evening instead of a boring time of hanging out with loser college girls. He expected her to put out. She panicked, punched his nose, and succeeded in breaking it. He began cussing and crying as he held his nose with blood spurting out between his fingers.

She ran to catch a taxi and arrived at the dorm shaking. That was the last time she had gone out with anyone before Sheldon. It wasn't until she was back home that she found herself again being pressed into the presence of men who only had one thing on their minds.

Her father resigned himself to her being home and decided that she needed to attend all the obligatory functions in place of her now-deceased mother. She had lost the only person she knew loved her while she was away at boarding school, and her father hadn't even let her come home for the funeral. She cried for a week silently in her pillow and did not eat for two weeks. The teachers began to worry as they saw her wasting away. The librarian was the one who pulled her out of it.

Ranalla had always loved books. When she wasn't sleeping, eating, or attending class, she escaped to the library and read book after book to lose herself in the arms of family, men, and friends who loved each other. She might not be able to have that life, but she could enjoy the ones that had it between the covers of books.

The librarian had sat and talked with her. She showed Ranalla that someone could care and helped her find a deeper love of stories to pull her out of her sadness and depression. Ranalla found that she could go on as long as she had an adventure or a romance to lose herself in.

Now she gazed at the man who paused in his work and returned her gaze. He knew she had been watching him and enjoyed it. She was growing weak, and they both knew it. Neither knew where it would lead in the end - life or death.

Chapter 14

Dinner was spaghetti and meatballs with shredded Swiss cheese on top. Ranalla continued to be astounded that her abductor was such an awesome cook. Between the books and the dinner, she almost forgot the scare earlier in the day. Almost.

The meal was enjoyable, and so was the company. They talked of great movies they had seen and books they had read. His knowledge of classical reading surprised her.

"You've actually read Jane Eyre?" She couldn't believe what she was hearing.

He laughed at the face she made. "Yes. I know it's hard to believe, but there are times when the classics speak louder than those written today. Then again, sometimes a shoot 'em type appeals to me more."

She took a bite of a meatball. Her face got serious as she gazed upon him. His enigmatic actions puzzled her.

"You confuse me."

He looked at her questioningly. "What do you mean?"

She laid her fork down. "You appear to be one type of person, and then you surprise me and reveal an entirely different side."

He smiled at her statement. "Never assume you know someone just by how they kidnap you."

She couldn't help but laugh. "That's it, too. This all seems so unreal until …." Memories of the helicopter overhead rushed back. "I still don't get it."

He reached out and took her hand. "Then don't. Worry about it later when you have to."

The rough skin of his hand told her he wasn't afraid to work. The soft way he held her hand told her he could be gentle. The heat radiating from him affected her in ways she had never felt before.

Nervously, she pulled her hand back and reached for her glass of soda. She needed something to distract her from her terrifying thoughts.

He allowed her to help clean up. There were still no sharp objects around. Just as she was not entirely too sure of trusting him, he was apparently leery of trusting her.

After dinner, they returned to the living room to watch movies. At least he watched them. Ranalla picked her book back up and lost herself in it. Her body slowly began to fade, but she was unaware of it. Vince looked over as the second movie of the night ended to find her with the book lying askew across her face and her eyes closed in sleep.

A smile crossed his face as he looked at her innocent and trusting face. Turning off the television and all the lights, he carefully removed the book from its resting place. Her mouth was open slightly and she was breathing deeply. He placed his arms under her and picked her up. She moved her arms over his shoulders and around his neck in sleepy abandonment. Her face rubbed against his neck and she sighed.

He closed his eyes briefly and took a deep breath in an attempt to get himself under control. If he thought it had been hard around her before, it was going to be a million times worse now that she seemed to trust him.

Even though it was dark, he moved around without difficulty. He had trained himself to be able to navigate through places in any condition, even with someone in his arms. The blinds were still down on all the windows and prevented even moonlight from getting into the cabin. After the scare earlier, he wasn't about to take any chances.

He sat her down on the bed and held her with one arm as he pulled the covers back with the other hand. As her head hit the pillow, he wondered if he should just leave her like that or change her clothes. Deciding her reaction would be worse if he undressed her, he resigned himself to removing her shoes and pulling the covers up over her. She sighed and snuggled down into the warmth. He reached out a hand to touch her face. A slight smile pulled at her lips. Shaking his head, he disappeared into the bathroom.

The night started off as the previous one had. Ranalla didn't move from her side of the bed. Vince stuck to his for entirely different reasons. As the early hours of the morning ticked by, both moved toward the center of the bed. Vince was awakened when a soft body shifted slightly against his. He groaned. Here she was spooning up to him, and he wanted to pull her even closer. He couldn't take advantage of her sleeping state, but the temptation was too great.

He began to pull away as his body reacted, but she surprised him by following and snuggling even closer to him. She draped a jean-clad leg over his bare one. He had forgotten that she was still fully clothed. A sigh escaped her lips as she pressed up against him. Her arms felt like vice grips around him.

His groan was deeper and louder this time. This was the worse torture he had ever experienced. He lay rigid and tried to think of a way to escape the situation without waking her up.

He felt her body stiffen as she began to wake up. Similar thoughts on how to get out of this situation without causing herself any more embarrassment were running through her mind. She began to pull back, but found her hair caught under his arm. Thinking to ease it out, she arched her neck and found herself face to face with him. His breath fanned her mouth as she paused in shock.

Though the room was still in darkness each one now knew the other was awake. They did not move as the seconds ticked by with their bodies pressed against each other, and their faces just a breath away. Their breathing became more labored as they lay there torturing themselves.

Ranalla took in a deep breath. It pushed her breasts against his bare chest. He groaned, "To hell with it," and crushed her to him as his lips claimed hers.

Her arms tightened around him at the feel of his lips on hers. A shiver ran through her as his own arms surrounded her and pulled her closer to him. The feel of his hard body against her only intensified her desire.

As her mouth opened to his, he hungrily took it. Exploring every corner, he let his hands roam her back and slide under her shirt. As his fingers ran down the skin on her back, it pushed him close to the edge of no return.

He pulled back slightly, feeling her breathing heavy as she tried to gain composure. His own breathing prevented him from forming the words he needed to say. He took in a few deep breaths.

"Ranalla." He gasped. "Ranalla. I don't want to take advantage of you. I want to know that you really want this."

His desired-filled gravelly voice shook her to her core. She swallowed hard. A part of her wished she could see his face to know more of what he felt, but another part of her was too scared of what she was about to plunge into to know.

"Ranalla, I want to make love to you." His voice was raw.

She knew he wanted an answer from her. She wanted to give it. Was she willing to give herself to this stranger that had done more for her than anyone in her life? Was she willing to give her body to a man she had only known for a few days? Was she willing to risk it all?

"Vince, I....I..." She was still unable to fully form words. "I want you to." With those words, he kissed her completely.

Ranalla gave herself and tossed all reason aside. For once she was going to live in the moment and take the love so rarely offered.

Chapter 15

Ranalla lay with her head on his chest and drew imaginary figures across his muscles. Vince smiled and pulled his arm above his head with the other one firmly holding her to him. Sweat clung to their bodies.

Reality began to seep into her consciousness. She had just let a stranger make love to her. Well, not a complete stranger, but a stranger still. The first man she slept with was one she had not dated for months or even known more than few days, yet a part of her felt a connection that seemed longer than that. It all felt so right. Then why did this sense of foreboding hang over her? Maybe it was the fact that she had no idea what the next moment would hold. After all, she should have been dead right now.

He sensed her trepidation. Turning toward her, he leaned over and traced her face with his hand. It was as though he could see every contour.

"Are you regretting it?" he spoke softly.

She took a deep breath and shook her head slightly. "No. It's just a....a little strange. That's all."

He chuckled. "Strange? I don't know if it has been called that."

"I didn't mean it that way." He could hear the smile in her voice. "I don't know. I never really thought about how it would feel afterwards."

"And how does it feel?"

"Good. It feels good."

"I'm glad." He leaned down and slowly moved his lips over hers a she sighed.

She rubbed her hands over the slight bit of stubble on his face. "I almost wish we had met in different circumstances."

"Almost?"

"This will sound stupid, but you kidnapping me sounds perfect for this."

He laughed. "What am I going to do with you?"

Laughter left her as the question rammed home. "Good question. What are you going to do with me?"

He licked his lips. "Get you to safety. That's what I'm going to do."

"Am I not safe here?" Her voice took an edge of panic.

"That helicopter tells me that you won't be for long. They don't know where we are, but they have an idea."

"Who are they?"

He leaned down to kiss her again. "No one who can appreciate you like I can." All other thoughts fled her mind as she gave into the desire that exploded within her.

Chapter 16

After more lovemaking, Ranalla fell asleep. Vince realized he could not stay in bed all day, though the idea was tempting. He left her sleeping peacefully and took a shower. He found himself whistling a tune as he thought back to the wonderful night they had shared. He knew reality had to be faced eventually, but for now he was just going to enjoy the moment.

The light stayed on when he left the bathroom. Her sleeping figure was still under the sheets. He smiled as he quickly dressed and left the room. Entering one of the doors off the darkened hallway, he sat down and looked over the panel of screens showing him various points of the property surrounding the cabin. Cameras were located strategically within a five mile radius to give him advance notice if anyone tried to sneak up on him. Though his phone had not gone off with any alarms, he liked to look himself to see how everything was.

So far, all was quiet, but he knew that wouldn't last long. The helicopter had appeared much sooner than he expected. Why had they chosen to search this part of the forest? The cabin was made to look uninhabited most of the time. Periodically, men would come to stay and not hide their trucks. They would hunt and give the impression that it was just a hunting cabin. Yesterday, he got the feeling it was being looked at in a whole new light.

His head turned slightly at the sound of water running. A smile played along his lips as he realized she was up. He was tempted to go in there and help her wash off, but he knew she'd be embarrassed in the light. Better to give her time. But time is not what they had an abundance of.

Satisfied with what he saw, he left the room and locked it behind him again. He went to the kitchen to begin breakfast while she dressed. He hadn't taken two steps into the kitchen when the cell in his back pocket began to vibrate and buzz. Cold fear ripped through him as he whipped it out.

Alert

He had left the room too soon. Rushing back to the locked door, he pushed the secret entrance spot located on the top doorframe and rushed in. There on three screens were men in camouflage very slowly making their way to the cabin. From the cameras depicting the scene, they were just within the five mile radius. He had to get Ranalla out fast.

He raced into the bedroom as the water turned off. He pulled out a bag from the closet that already had clothes, food, weapons and anything else that might be needed. He rapidly checked through it. He pulled out another bag that already had clothes in it for Ranalla, then grabbed a sweater for her and a few of the books she had brought into the bedroom.

Ranalla, wearing her robe and towel-drying her hair, walked out of the bathroom. When she saw him hurriedly gathering things, fear slammed into her. "What's happening?"

He looked up, raced to her dresser, and pulled out clothes. "Here. Get dressed. We have to go now."

She caught the clothes he tossed to her. "What? They're here?"

"Get dressed!" he yelled as he left the room in a run.

Ranalla jerked off the robe and began dressing. She was pulling on her socks and shoes when he came back in with a backpack. He nodded at her progress.

Grabbing all the bags, he began heading toward the door. "Let's go."

"Wait." She wanted to make sure she had everything.

"No. I have everything you need. Come on." She followed him to the door next to the bedroom. Reaching up like it did with the surveillance room; he unlocked the door and pushed her into the darkness. It appeared to be a deep linen closet.

Vince flipped on the light switch to reveal shelves of towels and bedsheets. There was just room enough for them and maybe another person if needed. He sat the bags down on the floor and then pulled her tight to him.

He whispered, "Hold on tight." With his cell phone in his hand, he pushed a button on his screen. Ranalla squealed as the floor moved beneath them and lowered them below the house. Slowly the shelves that surrounded them moved upwards as they were enveloped by darkness. She had a death grip on him.

The elevator floor continued down for fifteen feet till it came to a complete stop. Vince reached out and put his hand on a dark wall. After a few seconds, the door slid open to brightly lit barracks. Once they stepped out of the elevator, it returned to the linen closet, snapped into place, and the light went out.

Ranalla looked around the place. Seven cots were lined up on one wall. The other side had rows of live computer screens. She approached them and gasped as she saw men in various camogear moving through the woods.

"Is that them?"

"Yes." Vince sat their bags on a table that took up a quarter of the room. He walked over, peered at each screen, and didn't like what he saw.

"Will they find us?" Her voice shook as she watched the advancing army.

"Shouldn't. I've got a few tricks up my sleeve." He motioned to their stuff. "We'll stay down here for a few days."

"Can we do that?" She looked around the room. It was rather large for the two of them, but being so close scared her.

He started to nod as his eye was drawn to one of the screens. He leaned down to get a better look at the men. "Damn!"

"What?" She grabbed his arm.

"Let's go." He grabbed the bags and handed her the backpack.

"What's happening?"

"They've got explosives." He ran to the far side of the room and placed both hands on the wall. The unseen sensors recognized him and slid the wall to the side. Another black hole opened up. As they stepped into the darkened recess, lights began coming on to reveal a long tunnel. Ranalla jumped as the wall behind her snapped shut.

Vince was already running down the tunnel. She gripped the backpack tighter and ran after him down the solid, concrete passage. It was wide enough for her to run beside him, but nothing more. She was getting breathless with a stitch in her side when they entered a slightly wider section. In the middle was what appeared to be a cart from an amusement park. Ranalla realized it was a high-tech one as she got closer. Vince put the bags he was carrying in the back section and took the backpack from her. Without ceremony, he picked her up and placed her in the front.

Ranalla was too scared to protest or even question his actions. He climbed in beside her and started the small contraption. It sputtered to life and began to move forward. There was very little in the way of controls. She wasn't too sure how it was supposed to save them until it began to pick up speed. Before she knew it, her hair was flying back and they were careening down the tunnel that suddenly was not full concrete anymore. Surrounded by natural rock, she kept her arms close to her side for fear of hitting the walls.

He pulled his phone out in front of him and pushed a few more buttons. She had no idea what he had done. All she knew was they were getting deeper into the earth. There were no more lights, only a weak headlight from the cart. Fear tightened her chest as her imagination ran wild with all the things that could suddenly appear in the dim glow that reached only a couple of feet in front of them.

Periodically, he glanced at his phone. They had slowed down, but he kept the cart traveling at a faster speed than she would have liked. Suddenly, he yelled, "Hold on tight!" She had barely grabbed his arm when she discovered why he had yelled. A sudden turn almost threw her out of the cart, and she would have hit the ground if she had not been holding his arm so tight. They continued down another tunnel, but were slowing down. Eventually, they came to a complete stop. Ranalla couldn't see anything. She could barely make out Vince's face in the light of his phone. He was watching it intently.

Without warning, he pulled her tight. "Now!" He pushed a button on his phone, and an explosion further down the tunnel sent dust floating towards them. The ground around them shook, and Ranalla, trembling, buried her face against his chest. The vibrations continued for what seemed an eternity. As she felt it grow quiet, she looked up at him.

"What happened?" Her voice was weak from the fear.

His face was solemn as he said, "We're buried alive."

Chapter 17

Ranalla looked at him with horror. What was he saying? They were buried alive? Why wasn't he panicking or something?

He winked as he moved the cart forward again. The dust was light in the air due to the distance they had traveled. She was still against him with his arm around her.

"What do you mean?" she asked slowly and deliberately.

"They blew up the cabin. I blew up the tunnel along with it."

"Won't they notice the ground caving in?" She turned to look over his shoulder but saw only black.

He shook his head. "No. It only blew up the barracks underneath and the entrance to the tunnel. They won't be able to figure out there was another way out. They'll think their explosions did it all."

She lay against him and felt the soft damp air moving past them. "They want me dead that bad."

He nodded silently. She remained in his arms as they continued on. She was too afraid to move.

"Where are we going?" She still could see nothing.

"This tunnel goes under the mountain."

She pulled back. "There was a mountain there?"

He nodded. "Yes, but the trees blocked the view. It takes us to another exit that we can use to hike from."

"Where are we going?"

"To another safe house."

She looked up at him. "They found this one. What if they find the other one?"

"If they do, then someone is helping them."

She swallowed. "I'm scared."

"You should be."

"Not helping here." Ranalla rolled her eyes.

He looked at her. "Sorry about that. But it's something you have to realize."

They continued on in silence. Although the cart wasn't traveling as fast as it had been when they started out, its speed was still pretty fast.

Ranalla grabbed onto the sides of the cart with her hands and held on tight. Their visibility of only two feet in front of her just wasn't enough. An hour went by before she felt them slowing down. She could see light ahead that grew brighter as they approached.

When the cart stopped, they were surrounded by stalactites and stalag-mites. The light from the entrance illuminated most of the cave. Vince turned off the cart, jumped out, and helped her stand on the stone floor.

He handed her the backpack and walked toward the cave entrance. He stopped in a small clearing and sat the bags down.

"We might as well rest here. We'll eat and then take off." He took the backpack from her and pulled out some sandwiches.

"Looks as though you were prepared." She took one of the sandwiches and an apple.

"I was. I made these after the helicopter went over. Better safe than sorry. If we hadn't left when we did, they would have been our lunch."

She nodded, then found a stone slab to sit on. Her stomach growled as she unwrapped the sandwich. She hadn't realized how hungry she was, but they had skipped breakfast.

The sandwich was gone, and the apple was half-eaten when she realized Vince hadn't taken a single bite of his food. He was laying back against one of the formations with his eyes closed. She crawled over to him and touched his cheek. He opened one eye and looked at her. "Why aren't you eating?"

"Too much on my mind."

She shook her head. "Nope. You eat. We both need our strength."

"When did you get to be so bossy about all this?"

"When you saved my life again."

He reached up a hand and cupped the nape of her neck. He pulled her close and gently kissed her lips. "Not how I planned today."

She smiled slightly. "I know. I know."

"Ranalla, about last night..." He stopped as her lips pressed against his, and tears pooled up in her eyes. "Please don't tell me it was a mistake."

He sat up straight and took her shoulders in his hands. "No. No, it was not a mistake. Ranalla, that was .....beautiful. I just wanted you to know that it meant something to me. It wasn't just sex. It was more than that."

Her eyes brightened. "Really? I wasn't too....inexperienced for you?"

He smiled broadly. "Sweetheart, I was your first. That means a lot to me. He kissed her soundly.

Ranalla lowered her head to his chest. "You know that I'm certifiable."

"Why?" He rubbed her hair and relaxed back against the rock.

"I'm in a cave with the man who abducted me from my bed, locked me in a cabin, made love to me, and then I ran off with him." She looked up at him with a glint in her eye. "I'd say that's certifiable."

"Yep. Probably." He kissed her again before standing up. He reached down to take her hand and pulled her up. "We need to get going. There's another cave further along this chain of mountains that we can make before dark if we get started now."

She grabbed the backpack without him asking and put it on her back. It was still rather heavy. He must have packed quite a bit for them. How long did he think they'd be hiking?

He picked up one bag that doubled as a backpack and put it on. The other he carried over his shoulder. He glanced back at Ranalla standing there. Vince walked over and gently touched her cheek.

"You ready for this?"

"Do I have a choice?"

He shook his head. "Not really."

"Well, then let's get going."

Chapter 18

The edge of the cave entrance was all rock. Vince climbed out first, then turned to help her get her footing. There were many crevices, but none were big enough for her shoe to fit in. They stepped into the sunlight and waited for their eyes to adjust to the brightness. Once that was done, Vince directed her attention on the path they were to go down. She could not see a path, but followed him trusting he knew the way as they began their trek from the base of the mountain into the woods.

Since there didn't seem to be any smooth path from the ground below into the hole-like cave they had climbed out of, Ranalla doubted that anyone could have found them. Their underground chamber had been about eight feet long and six feet high, but looked directly up to the sky. On a rainy day it would have taken the water right in without a complaint. She was thankful the skies were clear. Being trapped in a flooded cave was not one of her ambitions.

At the base of the mountain, Ranalla found they had to climb down further still. She carefully placed each foot on the same rocks that Vince had just used and held onto the side of the mountain for support. The further along they went, she was able to use saplings growing out of the crevices for support. Eventually trees were all around them, but they were still maneuvering down a rocky incline. Soon as they reached the bottom, Vince turned to help her jump the last three feet.

She rubbed her hands on her jeans and examined the thick forest they were now in. She had no idea where they were or where they were going. Vince pulled out a compass and studied it. When he was satisfied, he looked at her.

"If you need a drink or a snack go for it. Now's the time."

She looked at him with wide eyes. "We just ate."

Vince laughed. "We've been climbing down that mountain for the last two and a half hours."

Ranalla looked at her watch and gasped in disbelief. It had been over two hours. She followed Vince to a soft spot under a tree. They each took their backpacks off and sat down. Reaching inside hers, she found a well-stocked supply of food.

"Let's eat anything that will spoil first." She nodded in reply.

She pulled out two apples and two bottles of water. They ate in silence.

Once he finished the water from his bottle, he looked at it as though he would find needed answers in it. "Put the trash back in the bag. This is the last of the water bottles. From here on, we use creek water."

"Is that safe?"

"I have purification tablets in my bag along with two canteens that we'll use. There's fresh water in them now, but we'll need some from nature before long." With that he opened the bag he was carrying and handed her canteen, heavy because it was already filled with water.

"We need to get moving on." He stood up and grabbed his own backpack to put on. She followed his example.

"Do you think they know we escaped?"

"Doubt it."

She paused in straightening the pack and looked at him. "I hear something else in your voice."

He sighed and looked at her. "I've got a gut feeling."

"Well, what is it?"

He turned around and faced her. His eyes were hard and his face was set in frustration. "They should not have found the cabin so quickly. They should not have passed by so slowly overhead the first few times. They should not have known any living being was in that cabin."

Her eyes widened. "They were told."

He nodded. "That's all I can guess."

She shook her head. "I didn't tell anyone."

He laughed. "I know. Someone else did."

"Who?"

His laughter turned to sadness. "I don't know. Very few know of this place. I hope I'm wrong." Before she could ask any more disturbing questions, he turned to walk. "Let's go before I'm proved wrong again."

They walked for several more hours before Vince held his hand up. He put his finger to his lips to sign she needed to be quiet, then signaled for her to stay still. He moved on and was swallowed up by the descending darkness.

Ranalla knew it wasn't as late as it appeared, but the trees above them were so thick that they blocked out the sunlight.

Through the increasing shadows, Vince appeared with a relieved smile on his face. "Come on. The cave is up ahead and everything looks fine."

It wasn't long before they were settled in a dry cave. Vince left her alone again as he gathered kindling for a fire. The chilly night made the warmth from the flames a welcome addition to their temporary abode. Ranalla's eyes inspected the cave and noticed it was more like a deep indention in the rock. It was barely seven feet tall and went back into the rock about six feet before it stopped.

She pulled out the last of the sandwiches and some cheese sticks for them. They ate quietly and listened to the sounds of nature around them. It was the time of day for animals to quiet down and return to the security of their holes and nests. On the forest floor the howls of wolves and other animals she couldn't identify filled the air. A shiver ran through Ranalla. As a city girl, she was not used to all this. Scenes from the various horror movies she had seen began to run through her mind.

Vince noticed and shifted closer to her. "No need to be afraid. The fire will keep animals at bay."

"What about the two legged kind?" She was unsure if she was more afraid of a wild animal or being discovered by those that wanted her dead.

"I figure we have a couple of days before they even think we made it. Though I doubt it from what they blew the cabin up with."

She gazed into the flickering flames. "I still don't get it. I'm a nobody. Why kill me?"

Vince turned to her and rubbed his finger down her cheek. "Don't dwell on it. Let's just focus on getting out of here."

"You said a safe house?"

"Yes. One that very few know about."

She turned from the fire and looked into his eyes. The flames were reflected within them, giving him a dangerous look.

"You're still holding stuff back from me, aren't you?"

He wanted to lie, but the trust in her eyes wouldn't let him. "Yes. Yes, I am."

She stared at him and waited for him to tell her more. "I can't tell you any more yet."

After a moment, she nodded. "What's the plan for sleeping tonight?"

"Well, we each have a sleeping bag with us." He noticed her surprised look. "They are wound up very tight and small. It won't be the Ritz, but it's better than the ground."

It wasn't long before the bedrolls were out and zipped up together. He glanced at her when he was done. "I hope that's okay. It's going to get chilly tonight."

She nodded. "No problem. I don't want to sleep alone."

He smiled. "I was hoping you'd say that."

Chapter 19

Ranalla woke alone in the sleeping bag. During the very chilly night, she had snuggled up tight to Vince. Neither one slept deep. He was constantly aware of every sound or movement. She was too scared to allow herself to fall asleep, and the sounds from the wild animals kept sending shivers up her spine. As the sun peeked over the horizon, she had just drifted off to sleep.

Vince got up and looked around for any sign of human activity. As Ranalla stirred, he brought her some granola bars to munch on and some water. They both ate contemplating the next leg of their journey.

"How far do we have to go today?" She took the last bite of her bar and chewed it slowly.

"If we get started soon, we could make the safe house by noon." He began packing up the sleeping bags as Ranalla stood up from them.

"What kind of house is it? Like the cabin?" She picked up the wrappers from the bars and stowed them in her backpack.

"Pretty much. The way will be a little more tricky. We'll have to be careful."

"What do you mean?" She looked up at him.

"You'll see." He walked over to her and placed his hands on her shoulders. "Just do what I say, okay? Even if it doesn't make sense."

"Okay," she said slowly watching the intense look on his face.

He leaned in closer to her. "Ranalla, I can't stress how important it is for you to trust me. We are facing a lot of danger."

She smiled reassuringly. "I understand. I don't know what all we face, but I trust you."

They shared a lingering kiss. "I only hope I earn it," he said.

They started on their journey again. Ranalla could feel the previous day's walk in her muscles, but kept quiet. She knew Vince had enough on his mind without her complaining about sore muscles.

The terrain began to get more difficult to traverse. As they came down one small hill, they had to climb another one. Ranalla was in relatively good shape, but this was beginning to really test her physical limits.

Vince made it to one crest ahead of her. He was waiting on her to catch up. She had just reached up to grasp a rock for support in pulling her to the top of the steep incline when she heard the whirring of a helicopter.

"Damn!" He grabbed her arm and helped her up the rest of the way. They were still within a cover of trees, but wouldn't be for long. "Come on."

He took her by the hand and they began running along the ridge of the hill into the trees. Even though limbs were smacking them in the face, they moved without hesitation. Ranalla couldn't see a thing. She just followed where he led and watched the ground beneath her.

She heard a roar that didn't sound like it was coming from the sky. As it grew louder, she realized it was the sound of rushing water. The helicopter was gone.

Vince kept pulling her forward as he scanned the sky between the trees that reached her. They turned down the hill and rushed toward the deafening sound. He stopped suddenly, and Ranalla slammed into his hard back. He didn't move forward at all from the weight of her collision. She peeked around him and gasped in wonder.

It was the most beautiful waterfall she had ever seen. The water rushed over the edge of the cliff above them and thundered into stepped rocks. Water sprayed over the entire base of the small fall. Ranalla felt the mist on her skin and smiled at the wonderful feel of it. She didn't have time to enjoy it long as he pulled her forward toward the thundering water.

The water soon drenched her, and the noise so loud she couldn't hear herself think. She tried to shout to Vince, but her voice was lost in the roar. She wanted to know where they were going, but didn't have to wait long to find out.

He reached the edge of the waterfall and took a step on one of the boulders that the water was hitting at the base. She pulled back. Was he insane? Was he trying to get them both killed? He paused at the feel of her tug and looked back. She couldn't hear what he said, but she read his lips loud and clear.

"Trust me."

She took a deep breath and looked up through the unrelenting rain that now soaked her. Their eyes met, and she nodded.

The next thing she knew, she found herself behind the cascading water and pressed up against hard stone.

Chapter 20

The rock she was standing on was narrow. If she moved even just a little, the water flowing down the rocks streamed onto her. The hard rock pressed against her face and chest as she held onto Vince's hand and inched herself under the water fall. She knew they were going to fall under the torrential waters as the roar became deafening.

Her left hand tried to hold the slippery rock wall, but found it was more dangerous than just letting her hand press against the wall to steady herself. A damp smell filled her nostrils as she breathed in the moisture from her surroundings. She felt the sharp scrape of the rough wall across her check as she moved sideways.

Suddenly she found herself falling forward. The rock wall had disappeared. They were now in a small cave underneath the rushing water. Ranalla turned around and looked in amazement of their sanctuary.

"What's this?" It wasn't a terribly large cave. Just big enough for them to fit in with four feet between them and the surging water.

Vince moved to the far back wall of the cave and motioned for Ranalla to follow. He lowered the backpacks and settled down on the damp stone.

"We wait here." As she sat down beside him, he took one of her hands and held it. He gazed toward the light that came through the water in the form of various rainbows. "There is metal in these rocks that will confuse any heat seeking sensors."

She looked at him in astonishment. "They have those?"

He nodded. "And more."

She swallowed. "We'll never really get away then, will we?"

He turned to look at her in the dim light and watched the shadows play across her worried face. He smiled, hoping to give her a semblance of peace. "We're going to do our best."

"Be honest with me, Vince."

His grip tightened on her hand. "I am. I'll never lie to you Ranalla. I may not always tell you what you want to know, and may keep from things you don't need to know, but I won't lie to you. Always remember that."

She nodded back and leaned against him.

"How long do we wait?"

"I'll give it another hour or so. Better safe than sorry. I want to make it to the safe house before dark."

And so they waited.

After an hour and half, Vince crept out from their hiding place and left Ranalla alone. She hugged herself against the chill of the water. Though it was still mid-day, the atmosphere inside the cave with the running water was several degrees cooler.

He was back a few minutes later and began picking up their bags. "Let's go. It's clear."

The way out was as treacherous as it was going in. Ranalla held onto Vince's hand with all her might. She tried not to think of the drop off behind her and the rolling water below. Though it only took a minute to get into the sunlight, she felt like it took hours.

Ranalla shivered in the warm sunlight. Vince led her down the large stream away from the misty air. They began their walk and let the warm air and sunshine dry them off. After an hour of following the water downstream, Vince led her off into the woods again.

The hike seemed to be strenuous as they pushed on. Ranalla knew it was because it was only the second day. Her body was making its objections to the pace known. The stress of running and hiding didn't help matters either.

The continued on until dusk. Vince found a hollowed out section of a hill with a rock overhang that he decided would do fine for the night.

"I thought we would make the safehouse today?" Ranalla asked as she lowered her backpack.

He began clearing a space for a camp fire. "It's getting dusk. I wanted to put off getting there one more day, especially after that helicopter's pass."

She nodded. Though she wanted to reach the safe house, she also wanted to reach it alive.

"Go ahead and get the sleeping bags out and put together. I'll gather some firewood."

He walked off into the heavy woods filled with shadows. She couldn't help but shiver as the night began to slowly descend. Danger was everywhere. Fear was becoming her regular companion.

Vince found several pieces of dried wood that would hold them through the night. He sat them down on the ground in a pile as he scouted for smaller pieces to use as kindling. Once it was all gathered, he looked up at the sky through the thick canopy of trees. They had at least one more day of good weather ahead of them, but he had to get her to the safe house soon.

With a quick glance around, he pulled out his cell phone and noted the medium strength signal. Hitting a speed dial button, he waited.

"Well?"

"I've got her."

"Bring her to me."

"No. You come and get her. And you come alone." Vince gave the coordinates. "Alone or you lose her."

Chapter 21

When he arrived back to the campsite, Vince found Ranalla had everything in order. She had even pulled out the dried fruit for their dinner. He had to admit he was impressed at how well she had adapted to their life on the run in the wilderness. Most women wouldn't have done it so easily. His heart tightened at everything that had happened, and everything that was about to happen.

They sat together in front of a bright fire, and Vince pulled her close. The embers floated up into the star-filled night. Ranalla sighed.

"This is so beautiful." The crackle of the fire made her smile contently.

"Yes." Vince held her tight, but his voice seemed distant.

She looked up at him. "What's wrong? Worried about the helicopter?"

He gave a short laugh. "Yeah. That's it."

Ranalla pulled back slightly. Her brow furrowed. "What's wrong?" She shook her head as he opened his mouth. "Don't say the helicopter. There's something else."

He continued staring at the fire. "You're getting the raw end of all this."

"I don't understand."

Vince turned and looked at her. "You should be in a posh hotel being pampered."

She shook her head and smiled contently. "Nope. I'd rather be here with you."

A look of sadness crossed his face. "Are you so sure?"

She nodded. "Oh, yes!"

Vince pulled her closer and softly took her lips with his own. The kiss quickly became more demanding as he moved her to the connected sleeping bags. The night became filled with soft sounds of lovemaking.

The next morning, Vince led them further north. Ranalla was beginning to get a better sense of where she was and the direction they were heading. The terrain was pretty much the same. Trees, rocks, and hills were everywhere. Chipmunks abounded in this area. It seemed like one darted out of their path every few yards.

Close to noon, Vince paused and looked around him. Ranalla was slightly out of breath as she paused beside him. He scanned the direction they were heading in. Taking a deep breath, he turned to her and took her face in his hands.

"Ranalla, do you trust me?" His eyes bore into hers.

"Yes, I trust you." She was startled at the words, the intensity of his voice, and the look on his face.

He opened his mouth to speak and no words came out. He closed his eyes as though trying to compose himself. "Just trust me no matter what, okay?" He looked at her again as though pleading with her.

"Vince, what's all this about?" She took his wrists in her own hands and held them tight as fear began to coil up in the pit of her stomach.

Harshly, he said, "Just trust me, even when you think you shouldn't."

"Vince!"

She gasped as he released her abruptly and began walking away. His words were so confusing and his actions even more so. She ran to keep up with him as his pace increased. Just as a stitch was forming in her side, she slammed into Vince's back. He had stopped suddenly and was staring straight ahead.

Ranalla moved where she could follow his line of vision. She gasped as she saw Sheldon ......

Chapter 22

"Hello, Ranalla." The greasy smile on Sheldon's face made her stomach turn. There was always something about him that made her want to wash herself just from his looks. Now she knew why. He was a snake like her father.

She looked at him in disbelief. He was standing so casually against the tree. It was as though he knew they would walk up. His perfectly groomed blond hair framed his tanned skin. He looked like the poster child for a luxury yacht magazine with his tailored grey jacket that he always wore. It made Ranalla think of Miami Vice.

She stepped back and found herself against Vince. Turning to him in panic, she saw that he stared straight ahead at Sheldon. Ranalla was confused. Vince was not upset. He didn't even seem surprised.

Sheldon's voice pulled her around abruptly. "Good job, Vince. You delivered her as promised."

Ranalla felt her stomach plummet. Her mouth opened and without making a sound moved as though trying to form words. She turned quickly to Vince hoping to find clarification on what was happening. She found it in his stoic gaze that remained on Sheldon.

"Vince." Her words came out in a whisper. "Vince, what does he mean?" Seconds ticked by as he continued to look at Sheldon. His jaw flexed as he gritted his teeth. Ranalla grabbed his arm. "Vince!" she raised her voice. "What does he mean? Tell me!"

His eyes moved slowly to hers. The look of sadness told her everything. She whispered, "You...." Her eyes closed momentarily. "I don't understand."

"Let me explain, sweetheart." Sheldon interrupted her. She turned around still in shock. "You put me in a bad situation when you ran out on me five years ago. I tried to get you to see reason, but you tend to be stubborn." He pushed up from the tree and moved forward a few steps. His hands were in his pockets in a self-confident stance. "I decided to use someone who would know you. Vince was perfect."

She shook her head even more confused than before. "I still don't understand."

"You see, I want you. Plain and simple. I don't like being denied. Through you I get a piece of your Daddy's action."

She looked back at Vince. "Where does Vince come into this?"

"You don't know?" His face showed surprise. Sheldon broke out laughing. "Sweetheart, this is one of your father's right-hand men."

A deep cold hit Ranalla like a ton of bricks. She slowly pivoted back to Vince, who was staring at her with no expression on his face. She struggled to breathe as she thought back to their lovemaking and his protective actions. All of it was a lie. He had betrayed her. He had used her. He was no better than her father.

Sheldon's laughter slowly subsided. "I found out what his price was and had him working for me while he worked for your father. He has been good over the last seven years at feeding me vital information. I've got quite a stash of information to use when I need it. The best part was his position to deliver you to me."

Ranalla still stared at Vince. She shook her head in disbelief at what she was hearing.

"You see, I get you and I can get your father's money. Everything is in place. I just needed you."

She didn't turn around as she responded. "You're wrong, Sheldon. My father has disowned me."

"That will change with what I have on him." He paused. "And when I tell him he is to be a grandfather."

Ranalla whipped around. "What?"

"A grandfather. I have you now. I just keep you in my bed until you're pregnant and then I have one more piece of leverage against the old fool."

Bile rose up in her mouth. "No. No way."

Sheldon moved quickly and grabbed her to him. His face was so close she could feel his breath on her own face. "You are mine, Ranalla. No other man will have what is mine." Keeping his gaze locked on hers, he reached into his deep pocket and pulled out a wrapped bundle. He tossed it to Vince. "That should be the final payment of what I owe you. I'll be in touch if I need anything more."

Ranalla heard the rustle of the package as Vince handled it. His voice came out tight as he said, "Glad you agreed to my terms about the money, location, and for coming alone."

Sheldon smiled as he ran a finger down Ranalla's cheek and neck. She strained away from him but could not avoid his touch. "No problem. You've proven yourself trustworthy."

"Good. I was hoping that would

Chapter 23

"Double crossing me, Vince?" Sheldon swallowed and pulled back. He still had a firm grip on Ranalla, but his eyes were on the gun.

"Let's just say I was never on your side in the first place." Vince's voice was low and steady. "Let her go."

"Got the hots for her? Is that what this is about?" Sheldon chuckled. "I don't mind sharing, man, but at least let me get her knocked up first."

A growl issued from Vince's mouth. Ranalla couldn't see him, but her heart quickened as she realized he hadn't really betrayed her. She felt dizzy from the sudden shift in emotion as the scene around her moved like a kaleidoscope.

"I said let her go." His teeth were clinched as he spat the words out.

The smile on Sheldon's face melted away at the seriousness of Vince's words. He took his hands off Ranalla and allowed her to quickly take a few steps back until she was slightly behind Vince. Sheldon held his hands up in the air.

"What's up, Vince? I don't understand." He shook his head and stared at Vince in an attempt to make sense of it all.

"Let's just say...." Vince's words were cut short as the sharp sound of a rifle echoed in the air. Instinctively, Vince reached out and pushed Ranalla behind him. He looked around for where the sound came from and where the bullet hit. It was only when he focused on Sheldon did he realize who had been shot.

Sheldon's eyes were wide as blood spread out on his chest. The dark red color gracefully moved from the bullet hole outward in evidence that he actually had a heart. Gaping at them in surprise, he fell to his knees before falling face first onto the ground with a soft thud.

Vince whipped around behind and looked into the trees. He grabbed Ranalla and began running in the opposite direction. She stumbled as she followed him. He was not slowing down for her.

They pushed through tree limbs and slid down embankments. Once Ranalla tripped and landed on her face. As Vince pulled her up roughly, she spit out leaves and dirt. He pulled her on. No words were said. They saved their breath for running.

No noises could be heard behind them. It appeared they weren't being followed, but that knowledge didn't slow them down. In fact, Vince ran faster. Eventually, he stopped so they could each catch their breath.

As Ranalla sat down on the ground, he looked around for any movement or sound. "You've got just a few minutes before we have to go again."

"Go where?"

"The safehouse."

"It really does exist?"

Vince looked at her. "I told you to trust me."

"You..."

He shook his head. "I'll explain later. Save your breath. You're going to need it."

Ranalla nodded. It was just a few moments later when Vince motioned for her to get up. "Time to go."

She followed him for another hour. They didn't run this time but walked at a very fast pace. Her side was killing her, but she refused to let him know. She wanted to keep up and get to safety.

Vince began to slow down as the trees began to thin out. Ranalla saw a log cabin nestled in an opening between the trees as she stepped around him. It was rather large compared to the one they had fled. This dwelling with only one story had a large porch across the front. The logs had been recently maintained and did not show the dark grey wreathing that many did over time. The front of the cabin had large windows that would let in the sunlight. Behind it was a lake that reflected the mountains, giving a breathtaking view.

He didn't let her linger long. He began walking up to the door of cabin. "Come on. You haven't had enough shocks for the day." He smiled slightly as he opened the door and stepped back for her to enter.

She frowned in confusion as she stepped into the coolness of the large living room. It was lined with the same type of logs as the outside of the cabin. At the far end was a stone fireplace with a moose head hanging from it. The furniture was all leather and obviously of good quality. It was the typical hunting cabin, though the size was bigger and the furniture screamed expensive.

She was about to turn and ask Vince what was up when she heard a noise coming from what appeared to be the kitchen off to the right of the fireplace. She looked over at it as a figure stepped out of the shadows.

Ranalla gasped. "Mom?"

The woman smiled hesitantly. Her pleasant face brightened up as she gazed on Ranalla. The jeans and flannel shirt she wore made her seem to fit in perfectly with the cabin. Her hair was now cut short and was a dark brown color instead of the blond her husband had forced her to dye it. Bright green eyes sparked at the sight of her daughter after so many years.

"Yes, baby, it's me."

"How? I thought you were dead." Ranalla wanted to run to her mother, but the shock of it all had her rooted to the spot.

"She should have been." The voice that came from the shadows behind her mother stopped Ranalla cold. With just a slight movement, another figure materialized. Her mother's face was devoid of the initial pleasure of seeing her daughter. Fear and disgust replaced it.

Ranalla glared at the new person. "Father."

Chapter 24

"Ranalla." The steel grey eyes of her father looked her over. "You look a little...how shall I say this? Earthy?"

She glared at the man she most hated. Nothing had changed with him from the last time she saw him five years ago. He still dressed immaculately, and a sinister grin possessed his harsh features. The steel grey eyes sliced once more into her soul.

"What is all this about, Father?" She motioned with a hand toward her mother. "I don't understand." Did he know about her mother all this time?

"I'm just now understanding it myself." He looked past her to Vince. A smirk pulled one side of his mouth to the side. "Surprised?"

"You could say that." Vince moved a little closer to Ranalla while trying not to push Gregory into action. His voice was controlled as was every action he took.

"I was too, when I found out there was more to you than meets the eye." Gregory's eyebrows arched up.

Ranalla spun around to face Vince. Her voice was raised. "What is going on here? Why is my mother alive? Why is my father here? What is he talking about with you?"

"So many questions." Gregory smirked. "Let's find some answers." He pushed her mother forward toward the couch facing the fireplace. It was only then that Ranalla noticed the gun in his hand. She looked up to meet his hard eyes. "Sit, daughter. Let's clear the air for once."

Ranalla found a seat in the chair closest to Vince. She had thought to move next to her mother, but her father had quickly taken that position while keeping a wary eye on Vince. Vince stood behind her refusing to move more than a foot from her. Gregory chuckled.

"What is so funny about you lying about Mom's death and now pointing a gun at her?" Ranalla demanded. Anger rose up within her.

"It's funny, my dear, because I didn't know your mother was alive. I thought she was dead."

"What?" It all sounded incredulous to her.

"I seriously thought Margaret was dead. The car went over the cliff. It exploded. I had no reason not to believe she was gone." The gun in his hand moved slightly to acknowledge his once dead wife.

"At your hands." Margaret spoke up.

He shrugged. "I never touched the car, Margaret."

She glared at him. "You didn't have to. All you had to do was order it to be done."

A smile tugged up one corner of his lips. "It can't be proved."

Margaret's eyes flashed at him. "Look at what you're doing now." She glanced at the gun in his hand. "I'd say you've touched the act this time."

"They'll be nothing to incriminate me." He spoke with confidence. He looked at her intently. "I need to know how you survived. The car was burned and a few scraps of your clothing were found. The investigation said the blaze was intense enough to destroy all DNA evidence of you being in it."

It was Margaret's turn to smile back. "Did a pretty good job, eh?" She sat a little straighter. "I had been in contact with the FBI for several months."

His eyes became hard as steel. "You bitch! To betray me like that!"

She raised her voice. "Me? A bitch? This from the man who didn't hesitate to beat me enough to cause internal bleeding multiple times? This from the man who tried to force me to abort his only child? This from the man who ordered my murder?"

"When something becomes a liability, you get rid of it."

"Something? A liability? I can't believe I didn't see the monster behind your charm when you courted me." Margaret shook her head in disbelief.

A look of disdain appeared on his face. His upper lip curled up in disgust. "You were too desperate and eager. You'd have believed anything. Which was good for me. I needed the funds your father had to get my business going."

Margaret shook her head. "I'm not that foolish anymore. I see you for what you are."

He shook his head. "Doesn't matter now." He looked over at Ranalla. "This could have been avoided if you had just given into Sheldon. You'd have been married by now and hopefully with a brat. I'd have some of his company and be on my way to all of it."

"That's all I was to you, Father, a bargaining tool? You'd have traded my body for more power?"

"You're my child. You're to do what I want when I want. Your body is mine until I give it away. Do you understand that?"

Ranalla stood up quickly but was shoved back down by Vince's not too gentle hand. She turned around to glare at him. He stood above her as though guarding her. She was so confused.

"I don't understand any of this." She looked at Gregory and pointed at her mother. "You order her killed. She lives somehow. You order me to give myself to Sheldon. Then I'm kidnapped with someone trying to kill me. Then I'm handed to Sheldon." She turned accusingly to Vince. "Then I'm saved from Sheldon. Then I find my mother with my father sticking a gun in her back." She turned back around. "What the hell is going on?"

Her father turned to Margaret with raised eyebrows. "Yes, how did you get away again? We got off that topic."

"It was the FBI. They rigged the car to drive off the cliff without me while it appeared to be me. It was my suitcase they found in the car. I've been in hiding ever since."

"I'll have to fire a few men for failing to do the job right. They ran a rigged car off the road. Idiots!" He turned to his daughter. "Now about you."

His eyes darted to Vince. "Why isn't she dead? I ask for a simple task and now twice I have found my orders ignored."

Ranalla's body became cold. She froze where she sat as the words sunk in. She turned to face Vince. "You? You were the one to kill me?"

Vince met her eyes with his steady gaze. "Yes."

Chapter 25

Tears welled up in Ranalla's eyes. Her chest hurt, and her heart felt as though it was breaking. She couldn't breathe as she gazed up into his steady eyes. Looking deep, she searched for a sign of him lying, but his eyes told her otherwise.

"You." Her voice cracked. "I trusted you."

His eyes never wavered as they looked hard into hers.

Her father spoke. "Maybe you will have learned a lesson how not to trust anyone, especially someone like him."

Ranalla turned around at the tone Gregory had taken. He was standing up, pointing the gun at Vince this time. He took a step back and motioned for Ranalla with the free hand. "Move by your mother." He never took his eyes off the other man.

With her mouth hanging open at the sudden switch of her father's focus, she moved to her mother's outstretched arms. Vince was standing straighter. His expression was still bland as he watched the man holding the gun pointed at him.

"Think I wouldn't figure it out, Vince?" Her father smirked. "Though I have to admit you had me fooled for a very long time."

Vince shrugged.

"I'm trying to piece all this together. Many things are still blurry. Were you involved in Margaret's deception?" He inclined his head toward his estranged wife, sitting on the couch with her arm around her daughter.

Vince didn't blink. "Yes."

Ranalla looked over at her mother. Margaret met her eyes and nodded silently.

"Thought your timing was a little too perfect. Were you in league with Sheldon the whole time?"

Vince shook his head. "No. He approached me last year and asked me to spy on you to see if you were aware of Ranalla's whereabouts. He wanted me to kidnap her."

Her father nodded. "Not surprised. He can't win her over, so he forces her. Sounds like the wimp he was."

Ranalla spoke up. "Then why did you want me to marry him?"

Without looking at her, he answered. "His father owns a shipping company. I needed the resources he supplied. You were my ticket to getting them."

Getting over her shock, Ranalla stood up. She looked with confusion between the two men. Gregory moved the gun slightly in her direction.

"Sit down, Ranalla." A voice expecting obedience lashed out at her.

"No. I don't understand any of this." She turned to Vince. "You helped my mother escape?" He nodded with eyes on her father. "You agreed to kidnap me for Sheldon?" Again he nodded. "So where does this plan to kill me come in?" Her voice raised with each question.

Vince answered softly. "Should I tell her or you?"

Gregory laughed. "You wouldn't come to your senses, child. You wouldn't accept Sheldon's attention. You wouldn't listen to me. I thought for sure you'd come back crawling on your hands and knees begging me for forgiveness. I never imagined that you'd land on your own feet."

"But kill me?" She threw her hands up. "Because I disobeyed you? Don't you think that is taking parenting a little too far?"

"You were a liability to me. Even after I knew of Sheldon's plans I couldn't risk it."

"You knew Sheldon wanted to kidnap me?"

"Of course, I had my own spies in his organization. That's when I knew Vince was working for him, too. It just wasn't until yesterday that I realized he was working us all over."

Ranalla shook her head. "What do you mean?"

"Dear Vince here is FBI."

She looked at Vince, who once again showed no expression. "Are you?"

Vince nodded. His eyes never left her Father's face. "When did you find out?"

"My informant told me about three months ago. I wanted to see if you would go so far as to actually kill her to get deeper in trust with me. I have to admit that I was surprised when she disappeared. I was expecting to get the notice she was dead. Then I was directed to a little house a couple of hours away where I found someone who was supposed to be dead." His eyes flickered to Margaret.

"You're good, Vince. You had me convinced. I probably would have not realized if I didn't have enough connections in the Bureau."

"Who was it?"

"Why would I reveal that now? He's kept quiet all these years. I prefer to keep him tucked away even from the man I plan on killing now."

"You would dirty your hands with my blood?" Vince asked surprised. "I wouldn't have thought you'd go that far."

"You've proven to me that I can't trust even the hired hands."

"You killed Sheldon?"

"Think I can't use a rifle? I'll have you know that I can shoot about anything, but why should I put my prints on a weapon? I prefer to stay away, but I see that this situation has to be done personally."

Ranalla shook her head. "You'd kill your own flesh and blood?" She was in shock. She looked over at Vince. "I don't understand you. Do I trust you?"

Her father answered for her. "I wouldn't. Did he tell you he was protecting you? Did he seduce you?" He laughed at the look on her face. "I didn't think you were so stupid, Ranalla. Seems Vince here has been stabbing us all in the back. Where does your loyalty lie, Vince?"

Vince blinked for the first time. "Not with someone like you."

"Figured that." He pulled the hammer on the gun. "Well, I have to get going. I have a business meeting scheduled, and I have to leave now to get there in time. Might as well get this all done."

"How do you plan on explaining all this?"

"Why, you are the one to kill them. I figure your involvement with Sheldon will help make it all the more believable that you would go off the deep end and shoot these two helpless women who were running from a rogue employee of mine who seems to have had a dark past and present I was unaware of."

Vince nodded. "Makes sense."

Her father motioned for Vince to move toward the women. "You get over there. It will make this easier to get this done with."

"Forensics will show how I could not have done this." Vince pointed out.

"That is why I have connections." He smiled.

As he raised the gun up and aimed at Vince's head, the windows burst in. Vince's body fell on the women as glass flew through the air. A scream rent the air as Ranalla felt something warm and wet flow down her face.

Chapter 26

The sound of the shattering glass died and silence took over. Ranalla could hear her own heart beating loudly. The weight of Vince's body pressed her into the couch. After what seemed like hours, she felt him move, which gave her a rush of fresh air. She changed position slowly as she looked around to gauge what had happened.

As he pulled back, Vince pulled himself off of Margaret, too. He had thrown himself over them as he caught a glimpse of the dark figures moving quickly toward the house. The flying glass soon followed.

Ranalla sat up and looked at her mother's bewildered face. Margaret gasped as she looked at Ranalla. Blood poured from a gash on her forehead from glass that had found its way to her. Her mother reached out to wipe the blood from Ranalla's face. Ranalla shook her head and looked around.

She saw Vince sprinting out of the room and through the door that led into the kitchen and to a back door. Pulling her eyes from his retreating back she was drawn to the various figures pouring into the front of the house that had been destroyed. Assault rifles were pointed in every direction. One man who appeared to be the leader motioned for two men to check out the right side where the kitchen was and others to check out the hallway that led to the bedrooms.

The same man moved forward toward the women who were visibly shaken. They stood up from the couch as the man reached up to remove his dark mask. A smiling face emerged. "Are you ladies okay?"

Margaret and Ranalla nodded. "What happened?" Margaret asked in shock.

"You're safe now." He turned to acknowledge the all clear from the others in the rescue team. "Come on. Let's get you out of here." He reached out to take each woman by the arm.

Ranalla looked over her shoulder toward the door she last saw Vince. Where had he gone?

Vince saw the men moving forward out of the corner of his eye. He only needed a second more of her father's attention to be distracted. He was given it.

As her father moved his finger to pull the trigger, Vince threw himself on the two women beside him. He had barely got them covered as he felt the glass fly forward. Pieces found themselves buried in his back as he threw himself on the women. As the noise of the shattering glass died down, he raised his head, where it rested on Ranalla, to see her father running out the back door located in the kitchen.

Without another thought, he shoved himself up and began running after the fleeing man.

He raced out the door into the bright sunlight as the sounds of rescuing footsteps could be heard in the living room. The figure of her father moved quickly into the thick woods. Vince caught a glimpse of his bright jacket.

Increasing his speed, he moved forward and pulled the gun out of his back pants where he had left it to surprise her father.

The tree limbs swayed where the older man had shoved them aside. Vince followed the trail with increasing speed. His breathing became labored as he topped a small rise. Coming down off of it, he stopped short as he found the end of a gun pointed at him.

Her father stood smiling behind the weapon. "I knew you were good. That's why I hired you. In fact, you seemed almost too good. Now I know why."

Vince breathed heavy from his run. "Pull the trigger. Why wait?"

"Just one question."

"What?"

"Why? Which one of my projects was the reason you deceived me?"

Vince smiled. "None of them."

"What? None? Then why?"

"Margaret asked that we save her daughter."

"All of this for that worthless piece of crap?"

Vince raised himself up straight. "Need I say more."

"No, you don't."

Birds flew from the trees above at the sound of the gunshot.

Chapter 27

Ranalla and Margaret found themselves sitting in a sterile room with only a table and its six chairs before them. Nothing hung on the concrete walls of the stereotypical police room. Ranalla sighed as she looked at the weary face of her resurrected mother.

They had been taken out of the once safe house and hurried into one of the dark vehicles that had rushed forward when the place was secure. As they left the house behind and made their way to the van, Ranalla turned around and tried to catch a glimpse of where Vince had gone. She saw nothing but trees and moving men in black with assault rifles and phones pressed to their ears. Margaret climbed into the van. Ranalla strained to look for Vince, but the man in charge, located behind her, pushed her forward and closed the door on the huddled women.

Within an hour, they had arrived at a plain official building where they were quickly ushered from the van into the room they now sat in. Minutes passed, then the door opened to a doctor and two nurses who came in to examine the mother and daughter. The exam didn't take long, and the doctor proclaimed them healthy. The guard outside the door was heard telling the doctor that when he was done, he was to report to another room down the hallway before leaving.

The women sat side by side on one side of the table. They clasped their hands together. They were silent as what all had transpired began to sink in. Ranalla's hand tightened the grip on her mother's, and she turned toward her with tears in her eyes.

"I'm so sorry, Mom."

Margaret blinked. "Whatever for?"

"If I had known you were alive, I'd have looked for you."

"Forget it, Ranalla. You were safer living your life the way you were. Or at least I thought so. Now, I'm not so sure."

"How could Father have been so cruel?"

"He always was. I just didn't realize it until it was too late, and I was his wife."

Before anything more could be said, the door opened. In stepped a man in a three-piece suit. He smiled and walked toward the woman with his hand out.

"I'm Agent Conrad. Glad to meet you both. And very glad you are both unharmed." He sat down on the other side of the table from them. "Margaret, if I may, now that the truth about you is out we need to make a decision on whether or not you are to stay in protective custody, or if you are ready to assume your original name and life with your daughter."

"Can she go into protection with me?" Margaret asked.

He looked over at Ranalla and smiled. "Yes, she can, but now that everything has been exposed and laid open, there are more options for you both."

The women looked at each other confused.

Agent Conrad continued. "You see, with your husband now out of the picture, that leaves his estate to you, Margaret."

"What do you mean out of the pictures? Is he dead?"

"No. Actually, he is in our custody now. He will be going to trial and will probably never see the outside of the prison again. That means, Margaret, that you now have control."

"I still don't understand."

Ranalla spoke up. "What would she get? Doesn't everything have to be confiscated or such?"

"Only the parts that were part of his illegal operations. All homes, most cars, one of the private planes, and one branch of his business were all legitimate. Those we can release to you."

"All his homes?"

"Yes."

Ranalla looked at her mother. "Mom, that includes the one in the mountains, the beach house, and the one in the Caribbean."

"He has all those? I never knew that." Ranalla nodded in response.

She then turned to the FBI man and asked, "What business did he have that would have been legit?"

"Seems about two years ago he bought an old bookstore downtown. He did nothing with it. Just bought it and let it run itself as it had before." He winked at her.

Ranalla gasped. Her father had bought the store she worked in. She had never really escaped him. Yet now her mother owned that very business. "You said he was in custody?"

"Yes. He is down the hall, where he is waiting on transportation to a secure facility."

Margaret looked at Ranalla and smiled. "Agent, may I see him?"

"Of course." He stood up.

Ranalla stood up along with her mother grabbing her hands tightly. "Mom, do you really want to do this?"

"Yes. There is something I need to tell him. You stay here. I don't ever want him to see you again. I want you safe from even his evil look."

Margaret followed the man out of the door leaving Ranalla alone, trying to understand how her and her mother's life had just changed.

Conrad led Margaret down the hall. They passed three doors before stopping in front of a windowless one with two armed guards on the outside at full alert. Conrad opened the door and stepped back to allow Margaret to enter the room.

Her husband sat at the far end of the room at a table similar to the one she had just left Ranalla at. He was not the man she had last seen. He seemed to have lost weight just in the few hours since he held a gun on her. His skin was pale and drawn. His lips were pinched. An aura of dejection surrounded him. She noticed a sling holding his arm up.

"Are you going to say anything or just stand there and look stupid?" His face was weary and ashen but his voice was as venomous as ever.

"Oh, I plan to say a lot." She moved forward. "What happened to your arm?"

"Are you suddenly caring?" He shrugged and grimaced at the pain that it brought to him. "I'm shot. Never thought I'd see the day it would happen, but at least I didn't go down alone."

"Where's Vince?" Margaret asked suddenly worried from the words he spoke.

"Last I saw of the snake was him lying on the ground bleeding like a stuck pig. He deserved worse."

Margaret bit the inside of her lip as she controlled herself so he could not see how she really felt.

"So, what are you hear for? To gloat at my arrest?"

"Actually, I came to tell you something."

"Get on with it. I have to go to prison soon."

She smiled with a look of secrecy and moved forward. Showing no fear of being close to the man, she leaned down to whisper in his ear. Conrad opened the door to see the look on the prisoner's face change from arrogance to shock. His mouth moving wordlessly. Margaret pulled back and smiled into his face.

"So long, Gregory."

Chapter 28

R analla paced the empty room. Her mother had been gone for quite some time, and she was worried. Now that she had found her mother again, she worried whenever she was out of her sight. The door opened. Ranalla paused to see who entered. She let her breath out when Conrad walked in with her mother. She rushed forward. Margaret pulled her daughter close and held her.

"He's gone. No more do we have to deal with him."

Ranalla nodded. "What about Vince?" She turned to Conrad. "Where is Vince?"

He looked confused. "Vince who?"

"Vincent Demarte. He was the one who kidnapped me and then saved me. He was the one who worked for my father but helped mom survive." Her rambling caused Conrad to crease his forehead.

"I have no idea who you are talking about."

Margaret laid a hand on Ranalla's arm. "Dear, let the agent get back to work."

Ranalla jerked her arm away. "No. I want answers." She turned to her mother. "You knew him. He helped you escape."

"Yes, but I also know what he was." Margaret nodded at Conrad who then slipped out the door.

"Mom, where is he?"

Margaret bit her lip. "I don't know. I do know that he was hurt. Beyond that I don't know."

"Hurt? How bad? Is he in the hospital? Where is he?" Ranalla's voice raised with each question.

"Ranalla, calm down. I know nothing more. What I can tell you is that you have to go on."

"What do you mean 'go on'? He's dead?" All color left her face.

"Vince lives in the undercover world, Ranalla. I'm surprised you knew his real name. Though he usually uses a variation of it, I'm told he typically changes it. He was known to your father as Vince Gregorian." She directed her daughter to a chair to sit down.

"I doubt you'll ever see him again. Even if he is alive, he is one that always lives as someone else. His life is not his own. Alive, he is in other worlds. Dead....." Margaret hoped the young man was alive, but knew the reality of it.

"Mom, I loved him." There. The words were out. She loved him. Now, he was gone. Dead or someone she would never find. "I love him."

Margaret smiled as tears pooled in her eyes. "I'm sorry, dear. But we have to move on with our lives. If he appears again, then you can tell him that." She sat across from Ranalla and took her hands in her own. "Now, I have to ask you something."

Ranalla nodded.

"Will you help me run the business we now own?"

"Sure."

"Will you help me manage the estates?"

"Sure. Of course, Mom. You don't need to ask me that. You're not getting rid of me."

"Good. I need you. Your brother needs you."

Ranalla froze and looked at her mother. "Brother? I don't have a brother."

"Actually, you do. When I was to die, I didn't realize I was pregnant. It wasn't until after the FBI got me to safety that I realized that I was to have a baby. I have to admit that I wasn't pleased with the news. I wanted nothing of that snake, but the baby could not be blamed for the evil of his father. I had a beautiful boy. I named him Randall, after you."

"I have a brother?" Ranalla's eyes brightened. "He would be...."

"Eight years old going on eighteen." Margaret laughed. "You'll love him. He's bright. He's funny. He's the son your father would have wanted, and now won't have."

"You told him? That's where you went?"

"Yes. I wanted him to know what he had truly lost. He could have had a beautiful and intelligent daughter, and a son to train in the family business. Instead he will have to fend off a few eager admirers behind bars."

"When can I meet Randall?"

"We can go now. We'll pick him up and head to our new home. We have some purging to do."

Chapter 29

The days flew by. As the newly reunited family took up residence in the country home that Margaret's husband rarely used. All items that belonged to the man were disposed of ceremoniously in a large fire that each woman gleefully fueled. It wasn't long before the cold house was turned into a cozy home.

Ranalla fell in love with Randall. He was a delightful child who discovered a close friend in his new sister. As his mother had said, he was very intelligent. Nothing escaped his notice, though he was wise enough to not always comment.

He was tall for his age with bright green eyes and a mop of brown hair that always seemed to need a cut. Margaret would cut it only to find it needed it again a few days later. It matched his ever changing face that reflected every emotion he felt. A turned up lip or an arched eyebrow revealed a lot about the young man.

Brother and sister found themselves spending every waking hour together. Even when Ranalla helped her mother at the bookstore, Randall was close by. Ranalla was pleased to see that he possessed a love books. He devoured each and every book he read.

The days passed by. Each one was new and exciting for the new family as well as sad. Ranalla never stopped thinking of Vince. She woke up each morning and hoped to find him nearby only to find emptiness. She longed to see him again. Whether he was alive or dead was still not answered. She had no idea if he was in her future. That was partially answered a few weeks after being reunited with her family.

Another morning dawned with sadness for Ranalla. Making her way to the kitchen, she felt her stomach roll. A sip of baking soda water eased the queasiness. She knew she should not have eaten that crab salad last night. It just didn't smell right. Looking out the window at the horse they had bought for Randall, Ranalla reflected on her future.

She was so happy to have her mother back and a new brother to get to know. Life was sure to not be boring. It was just going to be void in one section.

A noise made her turn around to find her mother standing in the doorway. She motioned to the glass in Ranalla's hand. "Upset stomach?"

"Yep. Couldn't find anything else to take."

"Good. You don't need to take anything too strong."

Ranalla shrugged and took another sip.

"Ranalla, do you know what you are going to do?"

She shrugged again. "Help you with the business. What else can I do?"

Margaret laughed and shook her head. "I think we are talking of two different things."

Her daughter shook her head. "What do you mean?"

"Dear, you're going to have a baby."

Chapter 30

The days flew by. As the newly reunited family took up residence in the country home that Margaret's husband rarely used. All items that belonged to the man were disposed of ceremoniously in a large fire that each woman gleefully fueled. It wasn't long before the cold house was turned into a cozy home.

Ranalla fell in love with Randall. He was a delightful child who discovered a close friend in his new sister. As his mother had said, he was very intelligent. Nothing escaped his notice, though he was wise enough to not always comment.

He was tall for his age with bright green eyes and a mop of brown hair that always seemed to need a cut. Margaret would cut it only to find it needed it again a few days later. It matched his ever changing face that reflected every emotion he felt. A turned up lip or an arched eyebrow revealed a lot about the young man.

Brother and sister found themselves spending every waking hour together. Even when Ranalla helped her mother at the bookstore, Randall was close by. Ranalla was pleased to see that he possessed a love books. He devoured each and every book he read.

The days passed by. Each one was new and exciting for the new family as well as sad. Ranalla never stopped thinking of Vince. She woke up each morning and hoped to find him nearby only to find emptiness. She longed to see him again. Whether he was alive or dead was still not answered. She had no idea if he was in her future. That was partially answered a few weeks after being reunited with her family.

Another morning dawned with sadness for Ranalla. Making her way to the kitchen, she felt her stomach roll. A sip of baking soda water eased the queasiness. She knew she should not have eaten that crab salad last night. It just didn't smell right. Looking out the window at the horse they had bought for Randall, Ranalla reflected on her future.

She was so happy to have her mother back and a new brother to get to know. Life was sure to not be boring. It was just going to be void in one section.

A noise made her turn around to find her mother standing in the doorway. She motioned to the glass in Ranalla's hand. "Upset stomach?"

"Yep. Couldn't find anything else to take."

"Good. You don't need to take anything too strong."

Ranalla shrugged and took another sip.

"Ranalla, do you know what you are going to do?"

She shrugged again. "Help you with the business. What else can I do?"

Margaret laughed and shook her head. "I think we are talking of two different things."

Her daughter shook her head. "What do you mean?"

"Dear, you're going to have a baby."

Chapter 31

Ranalla slowly became aware of voices whispering around her. She couldn't recognize any of them as they were too low. Slowly her eyes flickered open. A moan escaped her lips as she shifted on the leather couch. The coolness of it helped her come around.

As the blurriness faded, Margaret's smiling face appeared. Ranalla felt her mother's cool hand brush her cheek.

"How are you feeling?"

Ranalla slowly shook her head. She worked her mouth trying to form words.

Margaret nodded. "Yes. You did." No words needed to be said. Margaret knew the questions flying through her daughter's mind. "Let's get you up."

After Ranalla was sitting on the edge of the couch, she looked around for the other voice. The room was empty. Margaret smiled. "Get your bearings and go on the porch."

Ranalla took a deep breath. Nodding, she slowly stood up. Margaret stayed nearby until she knew Ranalla was steady. She then left the room to find her son.

Left alone in the room, Ranalla turned to gaze at the closed front door. Just moments before she had opened it before fainting. Now, she was to open it again. This time she knew what would be on the other side.

It felt like the longest walk of her life from the couch to the door. She moved slowly because she didn't trust her legs to hold her up. When the door was just a reach away, she stopped and started at the doorknob. That is all that stood between her and her future. Like something from a movie, she reached out and touched the cool metal of the knob and slowly turned it. She stepped out into the bright sunlight.

Leaning against the porch railing was a lean body that she had been yearning for. Hearing her step, Vince turned around and faced her.

He was a different man than the one she last saw. Yes, it was Vince, but he was different. A tired look hung around his eyes, making him look older. He was dressed in dress slacks and a button down shirt with a tie. Vince didn't look like a contract killer or a kidnapper. He looked like a business man who had just got off work. A suit jacket lay over the railing of the porch.

"You're alive." Her words were breathless.

He nodded. "It was close, but I'm alive." He smiled as he looked her up and down. "You're looking good." She saw a strained a look on his face as he spoke.

"I tried to find you." Her heart was racing.

His smile faded, though he still looked at her tenderly. "I know. I didn't want you to know where I was at first."

"I looked for you." Her voice grew stronger.

"You didn't need to see me in the hospital."

"They told me you didn't exist."

"In a way I didn't. Officially, Vincent Demarte died that day."

"You left me."

"So I could come back."

"Do you ever give straight answers? Who are you now? Are you playing me like you play everyone else?"

"Ranalla, I understand your anger. None of this was simple." He knew he wasn't going to get anywhere until he told her everything.

"I was born Vincent Demarte in Trenton. I joined the FBI. Nine years ago I was on the team who extracted your mother. We got a tip from an informant in our department who was playing the double agent that your father was going to kill Margaret. We had been talking to her already. So, we faked her death. That meant our inside person was now out of the picture, and she was adamant not to approach you. She wanted to protect you as much as possible. I was chosen to go in. I was given a past and sent in. Your father took a shine to me and I rose quickly in the ranks. Sheldon saw this and began his courtship of pulling me over to his side. I saw an opportunity to get more information. Gradually, I allowed Sheldon to convince me to work for him and spy on your father. I could tell from your father's conversations with me that he knew of it and was using it to his advantage. I dropped information here and there to help him and not let him know I was aware of his part."

"You left home and really caused problems between the two men's relationship. Sheldon used me to get information on your whereabouts. Your father had me spying on you in case you spoke with the FBI. Without knowing of the other one's plans, they each ordered me to take care of you. For Sheldon I was to kidnap you so he could have you. For your father, I was to kill you to protect his secrets."

"What secrets? I didn't know anything."

"You knew more than you realized. All you had to mention to the feds was seeing a particular person at the house at a certain time. That could be enough to start deeper investigations. You saw a lot of activity. What your father didn't know was that your testimony was not needed because I was seeing more than you were. That's when I kidnapped you. You know the rest from there."

Ranalla shook her head. "This is too unreal." She turned and walked to the edge of the steps. "So, you did save our lives."

Vince nodded his head.

"What about us? Was that part of your undercover act?"

"That's probably the only true actions of myself I have allowed in close to ten years." He moved closer to her stopping just shy of touching her. "Ranalla, I fell in love with you the first time I saw you seven years ago."

She turned around and gaped at him. "What?"

"You came home from college and walked in like a ray of sunshine in that dark and dismal world. Your father was a fool for not wanting you. I watched you from a distance. It was easier when both Sheldon and your father made that part of my job. I didn't mean to scare you, but taking you was the only way to save you while maintaining my cover a little longer. I just didn't expect everything else to go the way it did."

"You love me?"

He smiled and reached out with his hand touching her cheek lightly. "More than you possibly understand."

"You left me."

"I followed your father out of the cabin knowing you'd be fine. The confrontation didn't go the way I had planned. He shot me in the side as other agents came in and took him down. He'd have made his mark and killed me if they hadn't showed up when they did. I went to the hospital while all the loose ends were wrapped up. You had to get to safety. He had to go away. I had to finish up things with the agency."

"Finish up?"

"Yes. I resigned from fieldwork. I wanted to move to being a consultant for them and not an active agent who was always undercover."

"What does all this mean?"

"It means that I'm standing here on your porch as a man who finds himself changing careers and looking to settle down with the woman he loves."

She shook her head. "I have been wanting this moment for so long, but are you sure? Is this for real?"

"It's for real. Ranalla, will you marry me and spend the rest of your life trying to keep me honest?"

She smiled with tears in her eyes. "Yes."

He pulled her to him kissing her deeply. Pulling back, she looked up at him rubbing her hands on his face. "I was afraid you were gone forever."

"Nope. Just tying up loose ends."

"Speaking of loose ends. I have a few of my own."

Fear went through him. "What?" Was she really not in love with him? "Should I be worried?"

She whispered against his lips. "Trust me."